A Family to Cherish

Ruth Logan Herne

D0032789

Love Inspired

Recycling programs
for this product may
not exist in your area.

™ LOVE INSPIRED BOOKS

ISBN-13: 978-0-373-87755-3

A FAMILY TO CHERISH

www.LoveInspiredBooks.com

Printed in U.S.A.

Meredith shook each of Cam's students' hands.

"I wouldn't have believed it possible," she told the kids, "that students could work magic like this. I'd move into this house in a heartbeat."

"Really?"

"Oh, yes." She grinned at the girl who'd asked the question. "The bathroom remodel is gorgeous—I'd have plenty of room for all my hair stuff."

Cam and the boys groaned as one.

Meredith tipped Cam a smile that laughed at herself, and he felt his heart flutter once more, a sweet sensation of anticipation. Hope. It was a feeling he'd missed, but why was he feeling it now? Because no way, no how, was he tempting fate by revisiting old mistakes.

Once burned, twice careful.

He wasn't a starstruck teen anymore. He was a father, a teacher, a son, a home owner. He had responsibilities in their small community and he had no intention of forgetting that.

Although that smile tempted him to do just that.

Books by Ruth Logan Herne

Love Inspired

  Winter's End
  Waiting Out the Storm
  Made to Order Family
Reunited Hearts
Small-Town Hearts
Mended Hearts
Yuletide Hearts
A Family to Cherish

*Men of Allegany County

RUTH LOGAN HERNE

Born into poverty, Ruth puts great stock in one of her favorite Ben Franklinisms: "Having been poor is no shame. Being ashamed of it is." With God-given appreciation for the amazing opportunities abounding in our land, Ruth finds simple gifts in the everyday blessings of smudge-faced small children, bright flowers, freshly baked goods, good friends, family, puppies and higher education. She believes a good woman should never fear dirt, snakes or spiders, all of which like to infest her aged farmhouse, necessitating a good pair of tongs for extracting the snakes, a flat-bottomed shoe for the spiders, and for the dirt…

Simply put, she's learned that some things aren't worth fretting about! If you laugh in the face of dust and love to talk about God, men, romance, great shoes and wonderful food, feel free to contact Ruth through her website at www.ruthloganherne.com.

Or do you not know that your body is a temple of the Holy Spirit within you, whom you have from God? You are not your own, for you were bought with a price. So glorify God in your body.

—*1 Corinthians* 6:19–20

I have been threatened with bodily harm if I don't dedicate this book to our beautiful Lacey, a woman unafraid to get dirty but who cleans up well! Lacey is responsible for any and all family makeovers, she is our fashion guru and knows how to get "the look" just right. She introduced me to Solutions Studio and Spa and the "Fridd" family story, and bought me my first spa pedicure. The fact that she gave me two gorgeous grandchildren should not be overlooked, either!

And to Rachel Burkot, my go-to gal at Harlequin Books, an assistant editor who is always ready with a quick response, a get-'er-done personality and a nature that's sweet beyond words. Thank you for accepting the job at Harlequin, dear girl!

Acknowledgments

So many! First to the Fridd family for letting me invade their spa, poke my nose into back rooms, get a clue for the busy behind-the-scenes areas that make them operate effortlessly! And a huge thanks to Dr. Michael Haben of the Haben Practice for Voice & Laryngeal Laser Surgery. His cutting-edge techniques reshaped the plotline of this book. How wonderful to have such expertise in our own backyard! Dr. Haben answered my questions, and his honest and quick response gave credibility to an important background story. Thank you so much, Dr. Haben!

To my buds in Allegany County, Don and Karen Ash, who work constantly to promote the area, their businesses and my books! God bless you guys! Dave Evans, retired alternative woodshop teacher from Bolivar-Richburg High School: your work inspired mine, and I thank you sincerely. Your efforts in education are not unappreciated.

Thanks always to my family for their constant work to keep me presentable, somewhat organized and a little bit normal. My eccentricities should not be blamed on them. They'll get mad if I don't name them all (bunch o' babies!!), but in all sincerity I could not do this without their help and belief. Huge thanks to my day-care moms who allow me to exploit their children to sell sweet books. You guys rock!

Dave... Love you, Dude. Keep the tuna sandwiches coming, honey. They're PERFECT! To my day-care girls, big and small. Sophie and Rachel Calhoun are inspired by my beautiful young friends here in upstate. Yes... Even the "snarky" ones, LOL!

Chapter One

Meredith_Brennan@stillwaters.com

Talk about an oxymoron. Nothing about Meredith Brennan put a person in mind of still waters in any way, shape or form. Cam Calhoun ran a hand across the back of his head, wondering why his first love's name popped up in his business email box after all this time.

The elementary school doors swung wide before he could open the message. Children spilled out in an array of colors, overused outerwear showing the stress of a long winter. Kind of like him these days, more haggard than he'd like.

Need an estimate on building repair for potential new business. Phone 555-AGUA.

Agua?
Cam frowned, scowled, then sighed out loud.
Water.
She couldn't just key in 2-4-8-2 like a normal person? But then this was Meredith they were talking about, not exactly low-key. Subtle. Quiet.

He set the phone aside as his two girls raced for the backseat door, Sophie edging Rachel by a hair. "I win!"

"You shoved!"

"Did not."

"Did—"

"Enough." Cam swiveled in his seat, firm. "Sisters take care of each other. Not everything's a race."

Nine-year-old Sophie sent him a doubtful look while Rachel reached forward to soothe the line between his eyes. "It kind of is, Daddy. To us."

Cam got that. What he had trouble navigating was what to do about the constant competition between two smart, athletic girls, always one-upping each other. Was this normal? How would he know? He'd already consulted half-a-dozen parenting books and the answers were more confusing than the question.

"Belts on?"

"Yes." Sophie immediately pulled out a book, ready to immerse herself in the wonders of imagination.

"Me, too," piped Rachel. "And when can I stop using this stupid booster seat?"

"Gotta grow, kid." He winked at her through the rearview mirror as he wound the car out of the school lot. "Soph, did you have time to brush your teeth after lunch?"

Her guilty look said she might have had time but hadn't bothered. Would the Wellsville, New York, orthodontist care? Cam glanced at the dashboard clock, weighed his time frame, frowned and figured now was as good a time as any to call Meredith back. A ten-second phone call wasn't that big a deal, right?

"Meredith Brennan, Stillwaters, may I help you?"

His heart did a fifteen-year-old wrench that inspired memories of blue eyes, not sky-blue, but that shadowed federal blue he'd used on the Kinsler living room. Long lashes, without mascara. And soft brown hair, not dark, not light, like the shell of a walnut, new-penny polished.

"It's Cam Calhoun, Meredith. You sent me a message."

"Cam."

One word. One single, tentative, maybe breathless word and his head spun back to where his heart would never be allowed to go. Ten seconds in and he realized returning her call was a mistake.

"I'm glad you called. My brother Matt recommended you and I…"

Her voice trailed, uncertain.

Make that two of them, then. "You've got something Matt can't handle?" Her half brother Matt Cavanaugh was a respected housing contractor now, neck deep in building a new subdivision.

"Too busy. Can you come by and look it over? See what you think? Matt says you're the best in town."

He was the best in the county, but Cam let that slide. He didn't do great work out of pride, but necessity. Less than perfect, less than beautiful, less than right…

Those options didn't exist in his world. "Where is this place?"

"The old Senator's Mansion on Route 19."

Cam's heart gripped. He loved that Victorian home, the beauty and sanctity of the town treasure that had been empty for too long. "You need a house that big?" Instantly he envisioned a passel of kids running around, restoring life to the home.

"For a wellness spa and beauty salon."

Cam's vision disappeared in a puff of reality.

Meredith with a house full of kids leaving dripping soccer jerseys scattered? Meredith, of the perfect hair and nails, cleaning soccer cleats? What on earth had he been thinking? "We don't need a spa in Wellsville."

To her credit she laughed. "Spoken like a man on behalf

of women everywhere, no doubt. But I disagree and I need someone to help this dream become a reality."

Cam glanced back at the clock, saw he had over thirty minutes and made a quick decision. "I'm free right now if you're there. I'm about two minutes from you."

"Now?" Her voice hitched, but when she spoke again she sounded normal. Cam chalked it up to his own overactive imagination and refused to wonder what she looked like. He'd know soon enough, right?

"Now's fine," she continued. "I'm inside and the side door's unlocked."

"Perfect." He tapped the hands-free device to disconnect the call as mayhem broke loose behind him.

"The red one's mine."

"It's not. You lost yours, Sophie. I kept mine right here in the pocket of the door."

"Dad!"

"Dad!"

Ignoring the squabble, he pulled into the curving drive that led to the mansion's side door, envisioning prospective changes because he was determined not to think about what Meredith might be like fourteen years after she took off with her hairdressing license clutched in hand.

She stepped out the side door, a sweater coat wrapped around her. Was that cosmopolitan? Metro? Cam had no idea, but he knew one thing. She was still beautiful. Stylish. Her look fit the grandiose house and Cam had to haul in a deep breath, a breath big enough to push aside old hurts and wrongs.

They'd been kids. High school sweethearts that went their separate ways, quite normal.

Except when he stepped out of the car and released the girls from the backseat, he didn't feel normal. He felt...

Damp-palm crazy nervous.

But that was ridiculous so he ignored the upswing in pulse

and respiration and herded the girls toward her. "Meredith, my daughters, Sophie—" he palmed Sophie's head, her dark brown hair a gift from her deceased mother "—and Rachel."

True to form, seven-year-old Rachel reached out to shake hands.

Sophie hung back.

Meredith took the offered hand as Rachel beamed.

"I love your house! You must have a really big family to live in such a huge place! Do you have little girls like us?"

Meredith's laugh tunneled Cam back again, but he refused to be mentally transported any further than the house standing before him.

She bent low, meeting the girls at their own level, giving him a bird's-eye view of soft, highlighted hair, a perfect blend of sun-kissed gold-to-brown, pink cheeks that seemed unfettered by makeup and lashes that brought back too many memories to be good for either of them.

"I don't have kids," she told the girls. She reached out and took each one by the hand, drawing them forward. They went along willingly, as if she were some kind of designer-clothes-clad pied piper. Which she wasn't.

Right?

He followed them in, paused to shut the bulky door and turned in time to see her over-the-shoulder expression.

Talk about awkward.

He'd give her ten minutes and an out-of-the-park price that would push her business elsewhere. No harm, no foul, because the last thing he needed with outdoor soccer season approaching was to be tied to a huge job for a fastidious woman while juggling soccer games, 4-H functions, and his full-time job as a wood-shop teacher at the high school.

Ten minutes he had.

More time when it came to his high school sweetheart who was even more beautiful now? Wasn't about to happen.

He pulled a small notebook from his pocket and a pencil

from behind his ear, keeping his gaze averted. Limiting eye contact was better for his heart and probably his soul. Although there wasn't enough of the latter left to worry about.

Dream eyes.

She remembered Cam's baby blues like it was yesterday.

But it wasn't, and he was married with children so Meredith put a firm grip on the emotional punch she felt when their eyes met as he stepped out of the SUV.

The smaller girl clung to her hand as if they were new best friends. The older girl remained withdrawn, her gaze cautious, assessing her surroundings. She didn't look like Cam, but she acted like him, the hinted wariness offering another gut stab.

When they were young, Meredith had longed to embrace everything. Live free. Experience life. Escape the town that knew too much about her and her whacked-out family demographics: the cheating father, the drug deals gone sour that nearly toppled the family business. The illegitimate half brother who had the rug pulled out from under him. The workaholic brother trying to fix everything he could from a young age.

It had all been too much. Too dark. Too heart-wrenching to witness your family fall apart like that. Sometimes a girl needed a chance to start anew. Begin fresh. So she did.

Cam loved staying put, a hometown boy all the way.

Well, the joke was on her, because here she was, back in Allegany County. Who said God didn't have a sense of humor? "Girls, would you like to explore the rest of the house while your dad and I talk?"

"Yes." Rachel swung toward the stately mahogany staircase, expectant.

"Umm…" Sophie looked like she wanted to follow, but paused, uncertain.

"There's nothing they can get into?" Cam asked.

Meredith turned, met those blue eyes dead on and stumbled for words. "I...don't think so."

He frowned.

"I mean no. The house is empty. There's nothing here."

He directed his attention to the girls. "And you know not to touch anything, right?"

Two heads bobbed in unison, one dark, one fair, quite different but obviously united in adventure. Meredith couldn't help but grin.

"Okay. But if there's a problem, just yell. I'll be..." Cam shot a look from room to cavernous room "...somewhere. This place is absolutely amazing."

"Isn't it?" Mahogany-trimmed rectangular arches lay to the left and right of the center entry hall, while the broad, turned staircase to the second floor lay before them. Meredith moved to the expansive living room on the left and swept a hand across an antique glass window. "Aren't they stunning?"

Cam stepped closer and made a face. "But not caulked properly. And half of them are facing west. Big drafts in winter and spring. And they won't be up to code."

"Code?"

"Fire code. Building code. They're sealed so they don't offer an escape route."

"And bad hair *can* be a life-threatening experience."

She offered the retort lightly, but Cam turned a serious stare her way. "Are you planning a pedicure tub, like the one Heather's mother had?"

Heather had been Meredith's best friend throughout high school. Her mother had run a two-stool shop in her home and did mani-pedi's alongside. Sandy Madigan's gentle example had offered Meredith her first shot at her current career. She nodded. "Yes. Four."

"Blow dryers?"

"Yes."

"Curling irons?"

She was starting to see his point. "Umm...yes."

"Chemical propellants?"

She frowned.

"Hair spray."

"Oh." She grinned. "Of course."

"So multiple sources of heat and flammable liquids. Brett Stanton and Bud Schmidt do the fire code inspections for the town. They'll check thoroughly to ensure everyone's safety. Code is important."

"I'm beginning to see that."

"Listen, Meredith—"

"Cam, I was kidding." She sent him a more solemn look. "Of course fire codes and building codes are important. I just saw my brother go through all this with his new subdivision. I get it. Really."

"Matt's doing new build." Cam's voice took on a teaching air. "We're upgrading old. That presents a host of different problems."

"All of which drive costs up."

His shrug said that was a given.

"So these windows." Meredith ran her fingers along the wide, dark trim surrounding the old glass. "Can we modify them or do we have to replace them? I want to do what's right for the house while keeping in mind my budget."

"Which is?"

The figure she named thinned his mouth. "You either need a bigger budget or go step by step."

"That pricey, huh? Even with my help?"

"Your...what?" Cam faced her, surprised.

"My help."

"As in?"

She hoped he didn't mean to be as offensive as he sounded, but the look he swept her outfit said he meant it all right.

"You're kidding, right?"

Don't go all knee-jerk, Mere. Remember, he only knows

the girl you were. Not the woman you are. "I redid my entire place in Maryland. Not the skilled stuff like trim and moldings and cupboards. But the patching, painting, papering. New light fixtures. All me. I'm not afraid to get dirty, Cam, if that's what you're thinking."

His guilty look confirmed her assertion and reaffirmed her first instincts. No way in the world should she and Cam be working together. She decided then and there to let him bow out gracefully. "Listen, it was nice of Matt to suggest you and all, but it's probably better if I find someone else, don't you think? Considering our history…"

"Ancient news and there is no one else, at least no one who's approved by the Landmark Society. That approval saves a whole lot of time because they trust me to do the job right," Cam told her as he squatted to examine the floor. He frowned, scribbled a note, then rose in a fluid move that said he stayed in shape, a fact she'd noticed first thing. The dark brown bomber jacket fit broad shoulders before tapering to his trim waist. Classic blue jeans ended at camel-colored work boots. His hair was clipped short, browner than she remembered, but the North didn't get a whole lot of winter sun. His skin had a healthy look that made the furrow of worry seem out of place, but his eyes…

His eyes were the same soft shade of sky that melted her heart back in the day. *Gorgeous eyes,* she thought before clamping a lid on memory lane. His gaze proved harder than she remembered. Sadder.

Life could do a number on people. She knew that. Even when you thought you were chasing the right dream…

She put away that train of thought promptly. She'd learned a lot by being cheated out of the life she thought she'd have and the job she knew she'd earned. But falling in love with a married man…

With political connections…

That went beyond dumb. But only once does a person get a

chance to make such a colossal mistake. Luckily she'd smartened up, but caution and mistrust mingled as if they were her two new middle names.

Cam crossed into the formal dining room. "This crown molding is exquisite. You've got yourself a classic Queen Anne in all her glory."

"Meaning?"

"It's more elaborate than a simple Victorian," he explained. He swept a hand across the low, wooden panels framing the room and his expression took on a reverent cast. "The mahogany wainscoting. The gingerbread-trimmed second story. The wraparound porch. The turret on the north front corner."

"I love the turret." Meredith moved to the left and bent low. "The minute we saw this, we knew it would be perfect."

"Your husband and you?"

She grimaced at something resembling mice droppings. Closer inspection proved her right. "Mom, Grandma and me. I'm not married."

She tossed the personal info into the conversation easily because he was married, so her single state was immaterial. And that was good.

"Ah." He snapped his tape measure open, measured quickly, then closed it as he continued through to the expansive kitchen. "Do you hear the girls?"

"No."

He made a U-turn for the stairs. "Nine years of fatherhood has taught me that silence is rarely golden."

"Oops."

"Soph! Rachel! Where are you?"

He took the steps at a quick clip, then called their names again on the top landing.

Silence answered him. He turned toward Meredith. "Attic?"

"This way." She started toward the equally ornate attic

staircase at the end of the hall, but a giggle from the turret room halted their progress.

"Yes, m'lady?" Rachel's little voice had taken on a seven-year-old's rendition of peasant Scotland.

"I need proper biscuits, Higgins. These are quite stale." Sophie's tone embraced a more haughty British aristocracy.

"But cook just made them," Rachel protested, indignant.

"Cook's a fool."

"And the butter is fresh, mum."

Cam and Meredith stepped in as Sophie pirouetted, backlit by the bank of windows lining the rounded wall of the turret room. The higher angle of the March sun glared with little remorse through smoggy windows, lighting streams of dancing dust motes, but the sight of two little girls made Meredith remember another little girl playing dress-up. Pretending to be fancy and special. Above reproach.

That was a long time ago. When she was Daddy's little girl. Before the world saw Neal Brennan's true colors. And before she made the very same mistakes she'd abhorred in him.

"Daddy, do you see this?" Rachel spun about, arms out, a little girl twirl of gladness. "I just love it so much!"

"It's beautiful, Rach." Cam moved forward, palmed her head and leaned down. "And it's a perfect space for dancing."

"Kitchen help isn't allowed to dance," announced Sophie. She glided across the floor as if extending a dress out to the side, then curtsied toward her father. "Perhaps on her day off."

"Since you have an orthodontist appointment in twenty minutes, her dancing debut must wait anyway. Come on, ladies."

The girls didn't argue, but Sophie sent a wistful look back toward the light-filled, dusty turret. "It's like a princess dream room, Daddy."

"You don't like princesses, Soph."

Sophie made a face her father didn't see.

But Meredith saw it, and wondered why a little girl would pretend not to like princesses.

Not her business, she decided as she followed them down the stairs. Cam was obviously in as big a hurry to leave as she was to have him gone. He'd go, give her an estimate she'd politely decline, then go back to his wife and perfect family while she hunted up another remodeler to do the work.

He reached the side porch door and turned. "I'll get back to you with a rough idea. Best I can do with my time frame today."

Meredith nodded, playing along. "Of course. Thanks, Cam."

He herded the girls across the porch. At the outer porch door, Rachel slipped from his grip and raced back to Meredith, surprising her with a hug that felt delightful. "Thank you for letting us play in your pretty house. I love it," she whispered, head back, her gaze trained upward.

"I'm so glad, honey. Come again, okay?"

"I'd like that."

"Rach. Gotta go," Cam said.

"I know, I'm coming. Bye, Miss…"

"Meredith."

"Brennan," Cam corrected. "Her name is Miss Brennan."

"They can call me Meredith, Cam. It's all right."

"It's not, but thanks. I'll be in touch." He opened the side door, let the girls precede him and then shut it quietly without so much as a backward glance.

Not that she wanted him to glance back. She hadn't wanted him to come around in the first place—that was all Matt's doing—and seeing Cam's reluctance made her realize gut instincts were best followed. His *and* hers.

Chapter Two

Fifty-two hundred dollars.

Cam added the hard knot of financial anxiety alongside five years of guilt and figured he deserved both. If he'd been more careful, more devoted, a better husband, he might still have a wife and the girls would have a mother.

Somewhere along the way of being father and provider, he'd forgotten to treat life's blessings with the care they deserved. That carelessness cost his wife her life, made him a single parent, and left his girls with no mother to guide them or explain things to them.

The thought of more than five thousand dollars he didn't have raised hairs along the back of his neck, but he signed the contract for Sophie's braces and wished he could pray help into reality.

God helps those who help themselves.

His mother's tart voice rankled. He ignored it and counted his blessings. He loved his teaching job, the chance to show high school kids usable trades. Woodworking. Plastering. Plumbing. Basic electricity. He taught valuable, lasting skills to kids who might never make it into a four-year college but could do well in a trade-school environment. And to kids who simply wanted to learn how to take care of themselves with skilled hands.

He had a home. It needed work, but it was clean and bright, a safe and open environment for the girls.

And he had his girls, precious gifts from God, the two lights in an otherwise shadowed life.

Cam slipped the dental estimate into his jacket pocket, waited while the girls adjusted their seat belts in the backseat, and racked his brain.

The dental office offered a payment plan.

Cam hated payment plans.

He pulled into his mother's driveway as the girls started squabbling. His right brain knew they were tired and hungry and needed to run off built-up energy. Sitting in a dental office for nearly ninety minutes hadn't added to Rachel's humor or Sophie's patience.

His left brain didn't give a hoot and wanted peace and quiet.

"Stop. Now." He got out of the car and hoisted a small white bag. "I'm dropping off Grandma's medicine, then we're going home. Stay in the car. Got it?"

Sophie gave him a "whatever" look.

Rachel smiled sweetly. "Yes, Daddy."

Cam refused to sigh as he took his mother's back steps two at a time. Sophie might make her feelings known, but she'd most likely be sitting there with her belt on, reading a book or daydreaming when he got back.

Rachel?

She pretended cooperation, a winning smile under her mop-of-innocence curls, but she acquiesced in name only. Most likely she'd be chasing his mother's cat into the barn when he returned.

Fifty-two hundred dollars.

He shook his head as if clearing his brain, knocked, then walked in. "Mom? I've got your medicine."

"I'm in here."

Cam moved toward the querulous voice, fighting useless annoyance. His mother's perpetual drama had become a way of life a long time ago. "Hey, Mom." He swept the dark room a look. "Don't you want a light on?"

"Light hurts my eyes."

"Another headache?"

"Always."

He swallowed words that matched the irritation, not an easy task. "Did you take something for it?"

"I don't remember."

Oh, she remembered all right. They'd gone through a battery of tests last year as her memory seemed to fade. The diagnosis: old and ornery.

The prognosis: she had the Murray-family strong heart from her mother's side and might live to be a hundred.

Cam wasn't sure what to make of that, but she was his mother and with his sister and brother both out of state, Cam needed to be available. Although not nearly as much as she'd like, which was why he was getting the "poor me" act now.

He'd promised to swing by earlier. Meredith's estimate had messed up his time frame, but stopping by the old Senator's Mansion *then* meant he didn't have to travel to the other side of town *now*, at the end of a long day with two tired, hungry girls. Would Evelyn Calhoun understand that?

No.

"Can I get you something? Have you eaten?"

"I'm not hungry." She patted his arm with a weak hand and sighed. "Just tired. And I worried so when you didn't come like you said, imagining all kinds of things."

"I left you a message."

"Did you?" She thinned her gaze, looking up. "I must not have heard the phone."

Another trick he wasn't buying. She had caller ID on the phone and through her TV. If she didn't want to talk to the caller, she didn't pick up the phone. Which was fine until she used it on him to make him feel guilty for not being there long enough. Often enough.

"How did Sophia's dentist appointment go? Everything fine?"

"Braces. Pricey. About what you'd expect."

"I expect people are spending way too much money trying to look prettier, younger and thinner these days." Her words pitched stronger in argument. Surprise, surprise. "The way young girls slather on makeup and wear high heels. It's not right. None of it." Her voice accelerated as she climbed on an old but favorite soapbox. "Sophie's teeth are fine. They do the job, don't they?"

The girls raced in at that moment, and Cam couldn't be angry that they'd disobeyed his directive to stay in the car. It was getting dark and cold and his simple drop-off had turned into an interrogation. Or lamentation. Either label equated to something long and somewhat depressing.

"Hey, girls. I'm just saying goodbye to Grandma."

"Hi, Grandma."

"Hi, Gram!"

Evelyn laid an exaggerated hand against her forehead. "Girls, girls. So loud."

"I'll take them home. Get them fed. That will quiet them down. Kind of like feeding time at the zoo." Cam sent a teasing grin to the girls and they lit up in return.

"They've had no supper?"

Accusation laced Evelyn's words and Cam counted to ten—no wait, five. He wouldn't be sticking around long enough to make it to ten. "Girls. Let's go."

"Dad, did you tell Grandma about the pretty lady's house?"

"No."

"What lady?" His mother's voice scaled up.

Great.

"Meredith." Rachel announced the name like they were new best friends.

"Rachel." Cam crossed his arms and met her gaze, unblinking.

"She said I could call her that," the little blonde insisted.

Innocence painted her features, but Cam recognized the belligerent heart behind the facade. "And what did I tell you?"

Rachel sighed, overdone. "To call her Miss Brennan."

"You were with Meredith Brennan?"

"Doing an estimate. Yes."

"Instead of bringing my pills?"

He fully intended to wring Rachel's neck for plunging him into the heart of a discussion he'd be okay with having...never. "She needed an estimate and I was on that side of town."

"Why did she call *you*?" Evelyn emphasized the pronoun in a way that suggested any old woodworker would do.

Because I'm the best around, was what he longed to say, but his mother wouldn't get that. Evelyn Calhoun went beyond frugal and bordered on neurotic when it came to spending money. That someone would pay higher costs for Cam's expertise didn't sit right with her. But she sat more upright hearing Meredith's name, and the self-righteous jut of her chin didn't bode well for anyone.

"Are you seeing her?"

"What? No. It's a job, Mom."

"Why you? Why now? She's been back for months."

Cam grasped each little girl's hand in one of his own, determined to bring the conversation to an end. "Gotta get these guys home. Call if you need anything."

She rose, following them out, looking considerably stronger than she'd implied moments before. "We've been down this road before, Cameron. Fool me once, shame on you. Fool me twice, shame on me."

She'd used that quote all his life. Among others, most of them as negative and ominous as the one she'd just spewed.

And while Cam read the common sense in the message, he refused to be a doom-and-gloom person, and that set them at odds more often than not.

"You'd take a chance like that again, Cameron? After what she did to you?"

He wouldn't spar where the girls could hear. It was difficult enough to minimize his mother's negative effect on them and still be a helpful son, a tightrope he walked daily.

You hate it, his inner self scoffed. *Stand your ground, have your say and be done with it. Mark and Julia have no problem doing just that.*

That was part of the problem. His siblings had distance on their side. Cam lived a few miles away on a twelve-acre parcel he'd bought a couple of years back. Room for the girls to run. Climb. Ride. Practice their sports.

Still, he wouldn't argue with his mother in front of impressionable children. Reaching the door, they raced to the car. Sophie edged Rachel by using a well-placed shoulder, a great move in soccer. Not so much on little sisters at the end of a long day.

Rachel's cries split the night. Cam followed them, wondering which fire to douse first. His mother's intrinsic negativity, his daughter's screams of indignation, Sophie's heavy-handedness or…

His mind flashed back to the vision of Sophie in Meredith's turret room. Bowing. Curtsying. Sashaying around as if wearing a fancy ball gown.

His girls cared nothing for that sort of thing. Never had, never would. A pair of little jocks, just like their mother.

He grabbed up Rachel, hugged her, tucked her into her booster seat and secured her seat belt. He'd throw a frozen pizza into the oven and "nuke" green beans, the only vegetable both girls liked.

Then baths. Story. Bed.

Only then could he ponder the price tag for Sophie's dental

work. Work that would be essentially complete in two-and-a-half years, just about the time Rachel would need to start.

He refused to sigh. Or whine. Or beat his head against a wall. For the moment, anyway.

As he backed onto the two-lane country road, visions of the gracious Victorian swam into focus. Corner brackets. Framed ceiling lights. Muraled upper walls. Built-ins everywhere, a sign of a well-done Queen Anne. Shelves, closets, cabinets, pantry cupboards. This grand old lady had them all and he'd always longed for a chance to work on her, but not with Meredith Brennan.

Never with Meredith Brennan.

Chapter Three

"Tell me again why you can't do this, Matt." Meredith gazed up at her newly married half brother late Friday. She encompassed the entire mansion in a wave of her hand. "You said yourself the building's in decent shape, that it just needs a little sprucing up to be spa-ready."

Matt slanted her a no-nonsense look. "My exact words were 'it needs a doll-up and major revisions on utilities to bear the load of spa equipment.'"

"So..."

He stood his ground, solid. Determined. "Cam's your man. He's an expert at classic home refurbishing, he's approved by the Landmark Society, he's experienced and he's the best around. You saw what he did with the Kinsler estate."

She had, but... "I—"

"Mere." Matt grasped her shoulders with two firm hands. Sympathy met her gaze, but behind the kindness lay straight-up honesty. "I'd do it if I could. But Phase One of Cobbled Creek is almost completely sold and I've got Phase Two ready to go. It's March and we're moving into prime building season. And since my father-in-law is my partner—" his eyes twinkled into hers "—you don't mess with time frames that cost the business money."

"Money's not a problem," Meredith told him. Her bequest from her late grandfather had secured the sprawling Victorian. The just-upgraded loan from her grandmother would cover the remodeling. And hopefully a partnership with her old friend Heather Madigan would provide the necessary customer base, crucial to developing a new business.

"Not *your* money," Matt explained. "Mine. Outdoor construction time is finite here." Matt jerked his head south where the shaded foothills of the Allegheny Mountains rolled in splotched gray and white, stick trees poking up, bereft and dark, the late-winter look unappealing. "With the first section of the subdivision nearly complete, I'm already digging basements for the next group." He pressed her shoulders with gentle affection. "Stick with Cam. Unless you're too afraid."

Afraid? Her? Of Cam Calhoun? As if.

Meredith shrugged Matt off. "I'm not afraid of anything. I'd just rather not open up a box that's best left shut."

"It's business, kid." Matt's military training kept him on the upside of common sense. "And speaking from experience, we can't afford to let old wounds adversely affect business relationships in a town this size. We make amends and move on." He jerked a shoulder toward the rambling house. "With two kids to take care of, Cam could use the work and you need someone good enough to create what you envision here. I'm a construction guy. Not a fine carpenter."

His words tipped the balance. Meredith knew what she wanted, she'd envisioned the finished product that would allow beautiful but affordable spa luxuries to the men and women of Allegany County. The recent upsurge in employment and business made this move timely. Grandpa's money made it affordable.

But why Cam? Of all the craftsmen in all the world...

Reality smacked her. Wellsville and Jamison weren't that big. And fine carpenters weren't common in large metropolises. Here?

The local towns were blessed to have a craftsman of Cam's caliber available. She huffed a sigh, folded her arms and dropped her chin. "Okay."

Matt laughed, gave her a brotherly chuck on the arm and headed toward his truck. "Gotta head out. Callie's got a doctor's appointment in thirty minutes."

"Aha."

He met her up-thrust brows with a wink. "It's too early for big announcements, but prayers are appreciated."

"Oh, Matt." Meredith hugged him before he climbed into the truck. "I'm so happy for you. And a baby…"

"Not gettin' any younger," Matt told her, "so we decided not to wait."

"When?"

"Thanksgiving if all goes well."

"Perfect."

Matt's crooked grin showed his full agreement. "'Bout as close to that as you can get on Earth, sis."

He drove off, leaving her to contemplate her current predicament. Was she stupid to have invested in this old place? Or was she savvy to have recognized the amazing potential?

Trust in the Lord with all your heart and lean not on your own understanding.

Sage words. Sound advice she wished she'd embodied a few years ago before losing her heart to a man who led two lives, a man like her trouble-making illicit father. If she'd heeded her mother's wisdom back then, she'd have averted a lot of unnecessary drama.

A stupid mistake, one she would never repeat and would rather forget. She hoped coming home to Allegany County allowed just that.

Some days Cam hated that the cemetery stood half a mile east of their home. Others, like today, he welcomed the proximity. Once the girls awoke, his hours would race from one task to another, a typical Saturday in the life of a single parent. And then he'd play catch-up on Sunday, taking care of menial tasks left undone during the busy week before starting all over again Monday morning. But he refused to dwell on the negatives. His beautiful girls made the time, the work and the sacrifice worthwhile.

Cam would have said the chill morning fog painted the trek from the gravel-stone path to the gray stone marker in monochromes, if he was prone to drama.

He wasn't.

But the sigh in his heart softened his jaw as the etched words became more legible with each step.

Kristine DeRose Calhoun
Beloved wife, mother and daughter

The stark reality of the carved letters sucker-punched him every time. The all-consuming ache he'd felt those first weeks and months had dulled to an old sore, but he couldn't come to the graveyard to pay respects without remembering Kristy there, on their old couch, gone forever.

Irreparable harm. That's what he'd done. Not like he'd gone to bed expecting her to die, but he'd gone to bed cranky and bad-tempered, as if her time, her work with the girls, her tasks were less important than his. Sometimes that hurt more than her death, that he'd minimized her worth in sharp words that last night.

He laid the single red rose on the grave, a tribute to an old promise, when Kristy had scoffed at the idea of money wasted on twelve flowers, destined to be tossed away within days. "One flower," she'd told him, smiling, trailing her hand along his scruffy cheek. "Just one, now and again. To show me you care."

He had cared. Did care. As he stared at the single flush

of color against dull grays of the early-spring graveyard, he wished he had a chance, one more chance to say he was sorry.

So sorry.

But he'd blown that, too, so he leaned down, laid his hand against the cold, smooth stone, and prayed the prayer that remained unanswered, a prayer for forgiveness.

The hard, flat surface yielded nothing, but he was used to that. He straightened and tipped the visor of his faded baseball cap, but didn't wink like he used to when she was alive.

Because she wasn't.

"Meredith!"

Meredith turned from the display of nineteenth-century-styled tinware and laughed as Rachel Calhoun raced around two tables of carved wooden bowls to tackle into her on Saturday morning. "Hey, Rach. How's it going?"

"Rachel. Walk," Cam said.

"Sorry, Dad. Meredith's here!"

"I see that."

Cam's tone said she ranked pretty much last on the list of people he hoped to run into this cold, rainy Saturday, but she'd figured that out the other day. Meredith looked around, searching, then raised a brow of question to the little girl wrapped around her legs. "Where's Sophie?"

"Indoor soccer practice," Rachel explained. "I already had mine."

"Which explains the cool athletic look you're sporting," Meredith noted. Rachel's face brightened and she turned this way and that, peering over her shoulder in an unsuccessful attempt to see the number on her jersey. "I'm number seven, see?"

"It's a great number."

"Sophie's number seven, too."

"A little odd, but still wonderful," Meredith said.

"It was my Mommy's number in high school," Rachel continued. "We asked the coaches if we could both use it 'cause we're on different teams."

"A marvelous family tradition." Meredith stooped low and met the little girl's frank gaze. "Your mommy must be very proud to have two beautiful athletic daughters following in her footsteps."

"She's dead."

Silence yawned. Meredith swallowed hard, saw the stark honesty in the little girl's expression, and looked up to Cam for confirmation. The look of loss in his light eyes offered affirmation. Meredith gave Rachel a quick hug. "I'm sorry, honey. I didn't know that."

Rachel mused, then nodded. "You're new. And she died when I was really small. Daddy remembers. So does Sophie. And I kind of do. A little."

Meredith looked into this miniature version of Cam's blue eyes and read the wistfulness there, a pensiveness that suggested she didn't really remember but longed to.

Meredith's heart opened wide, along with her arms. She hugged Rachel, then rocked back on her heels. "So. Are you good?" she asked, nodding at the light blue soccer uniform.

Rachel beamed. "Yes. Very."

"I'm not a bit surprised." Meredith laughed and stood, then grimaced as her knees unlocked.

"Are you all right?"

Cam's voice actually sounded concerned, but that was because Cam Calhoun was one of the world's nicest guys. "Fine. My knees do not like that position, though, and they remind me that I'm not twenty anymore. Or seven." She smiled down at the little girl, then redirected her attention to Cam. "I assume since I haven't heard from you that you're going to pass on my project?"

"No." He frowned slightly, as though her assumption surprised him, but then why hadn't he called? Gotten back to her? It had been…

"It's only been two days," he reminded her. "And I need to get a better look at the upstairs measurements to do a full write-up, but as long as you're not in a huge hurry for the work to be complete—"

Meredith didn't clamp her guilty look in time.

Cam sighed and maintained eye contact using that assessing expression he seemed to have perfected. Patient with a hint of long-suffering that said more than words ever could. "What time frame were you expecting, Meredith?"

She flinched and admitted, "Six weeks."

"Twelve," he countered in a flat voice. "And that's pushing it. It's March. We'd be looking at a July finishing date."

"You're serious?"

"Always."

She smiled, his one-word answer reminding her that he *was* generally serious. And sincere. And heart-wrenching handsome, with or without his glasses on. And a widower.

She hadn't counted on that last fact. And while it shouldn't make a difference, she'd taken stoic comfort in his married state these past two days when old memories ran like creek water on a summer's day. But now twelve weeks of working together to get Stillwaters into shape?

"What will take so long?" His look of impatience made her rephrase the sentence. "I'm sorry, that sounded rude. I meant what aspects of the job push it to twelve weeks? The new plumbing? Electric upgrades?"

"My job."

She frowned, not understanding.

Cam tipped his head. A tiny wrinkle between his brows begged to be smoothed away.

Meredith ignored the plea.

"I'm a teacher."

Well, that explained those practiced classroom looks.

The steady gaze, the heightened expectations. "A teacher? Really?"

"Is it that surprising, Mere? It's been fourteen years."

Oh, she knew that. She'd spent those fourteen years working, training, finessing and climbing her way up the ladder of spa success only to crash when the spa owner's daughter decided her four-year business degree from a third-tier school bested fourteen years of hard-earned experience. Jude Anne Geisler played the trump card well, offering to let the world know that Meredith had been running around with Sylvia Sinclair Bellwater's husband.

By that point it didn't matter that Meredith had been duped by the successful businessman and his clever alias. Her fault, she knew. She squelched an urge to get even because the man she knew as Chas Bell had a wife and three kids who would be hurt if those allegations became public. Sylvia Bellwater didn't need to go through what Meredith's mother had endured. Not at her hands, anyway.

And she knew Chas would eventually be found out. Scum had a way of rising to the surface.

But it wouldn't be because of her, so she sidestepped the drama while the resort owner's daughter stepped into the management position Meredith had primed herself for the past five years.

Nepotism and her own stupidity put her out of the job she'd worked for, and brought her back home to Wellsville and Jamison. She lifted a shoulder in a half shrug. "I didn't know."

"So I'm working full-time until the end of June. I've got two busy little girls." He chucked Rachel under the chin. She grinned up at him, the wide smile flashing love and devotion between father and daughter. The exchanged look drew Meredith back in time, to another little girl, gazing at her dad in adoration. Only that little girl had been sadly misled. This one wouldn't be.

"And outdoor soccer season is starting."

"And they both play, which puts you in a time crunch." Meredith tipped her smile down. Rachel grinned up at her with Cam's eyes. Cam's face. Cam's light hair.

"Yes. I generally only take on big projects in the summer, so you're timing isn't good—"

She frowned, disappointed.

"And pouting will get you nowhere."

"That wasn't pouting. It was frowning. Huge difference."

Her quick retort made him smile, and the minute he did, fourteen years melted away in a flash of warmth. "Let's go with *slight* difference. More accurate. So if you're still interested…"

"In getting the work done," she interjected, then sent him an innocent smile.

"Exactly." His expression said nothing else was on the table, so that was good, right? "I can come by later today, finish measuring and give you an estimate. Then you can decide."

"I've already decided," she told him. When he looked surprised and a little discomfited, she went on, "I checked out your references from Matt, viewed the Kinsler place at length, and worked out an arrangement with Grandma for the loan. We're good."

"You're giving me carte blanche without an estimate? That's not good business."

"That's not what I'm doing." She faced him square. "I'm cutting a deal with a skilled craftsman who is known throughout the town as fair, conscientious and amazing."

His eyes sparked at the word *amazing* and if she was interested at all, she'd have thought she noted a glimmer of something not exactly business-related in his expression.

If you were interested? Are you kidding me? Did you not see that look, that flash of light in his eyes? Come on, girl, get back in the game.

"Cameron."

A cross-sounding voice interrupted their conversation. Rachel stepped closer to her father, and Meredith wished she could mimic the little girl's wrinkle of displeasure, but grown-ups were required to maintain a game face in public. Right now Meredith considered it a really stupid rule.

"Mrs. Dennehy. How are you?" Cam kept his tone easy while Meredith considered ways to put the meddlesome old woman in her place. Claire Dennehy had sharpened her tongue at the Brennan family's expense for a long time. Of course, Meredith's father had given the town plenty of reason to gossip. Gambling, drug addiction, womanizing and illegitimate children made for great backyard fodder, but Claire and Cam's mother had gone above and beyond in their condemnations, which meant Meredith's teenage relationship with Cam put both women in a tongue-wagging tizzy.

The fact that they ran into each other here, in John Dennehy's old-fashioned mercantile, gave Claire a new opportunity to scold, but if Meredith was going to make it in this town, she needed to toughen up. And Rachel didn't need to hear the old woman's caustic drivel. "Rachel, would you like to look at some wallpaper samples with me?"

"Wallpaper?" Rachel wrinkled her nose, puzzled.

Cam snorted.

Meredith ignored his noise and headed toward the door. "If it's all right with you, we'll head a little west on Main Street and see what Mr. Schiffler's got in Victorian prints."

Cam sent her a grateful look that said he recognized her ploy to move Rachel out of earshot, but the arched brow said they'd be discussing the wallpaper idea.

His amused look of challenge made her look forward to the discussion, a fact she'd examine later. Right now her big goal was removing seven-year-old hearing from the reach of a cranky old woman.

* * *

"I went to see your mother last night." Claire threw down the comment like a dueling glove, then waited for Cam to retrieve it.

He refused the challenge and kept his peace. "I appreciate that. She gets lonely."

"She'd be less lonely if certain people spent more time with her."

"Or if she went places," Cam returned mildly. "Did you happen to take her any black licorice?"

"No."

"Then I'll get some now." His mother loved black licorice. And black jelly beans. Anise cookies. She enjoyed the biting flavor of the spiced treats.

"She didn't look good."

Cam pointed to the display case. "I'll take a pound of the black jelly beans and the same of the black licorice whips."

"Her color's bad."

His mother's color would improve if she got outside more often and exercised her cheeks by smiling now and again. Neither option was likely.

"And she had a coughing spell something fierce when I was there. That will be nine-thirty-nine."

Cam handed her a ten-dollar bill, smiled his thanks, and accepted the small bag and the change she handed him. "Have a nice day, now."

He felt her stewing as he walked out the door, miffed because he refused to jump into a discussion about his mother. Their relationship, as strange as it was, was their business.

Not Claire's.

He shoved his shoulders back consciously, as if listening to Claire's negativity bowed him down. It didn't, but it could, and Cam refused to let that happen. Thank heavens Meredith had been there to sweep Rachel out the door. Rachel was too quick for her own good, and listening to ill-tempered diatribes wasn't in her best interest. Especially when she was adept at repeating things at the worst possible moments.

He paused, scraped a hand to his jeans, and eyed Schiffler's door.

He'd just thanked God for Meredith Brennan. What in the world was he thinking?

Obviously an anomaly he wasn't about to repeat. He entered the store just in time to hear Rachel exclaim, "I love this one, Meredith!"

Excitement highlighted Rachel's delight as twin grins looked his way, a glimpse of shared femininity. Warmth flowed through him, seeing Rachel perched on a tall stool alongside Meredith. The little girl's fair curls matched the soft highlights in Meredith's hair, and for one brief flash of time they looked like they belonged together.

Except they didn't.

Rachel waved him over. "Dad, you have *got* to see this."

"Whaddya got, kid?"

"Look."

He wasn't sure what he expected, but it wasn't the fussy border done in shades of pink and white. The wide strip showcased delicate teacups, doilies and china teapots in mixed floral designs. Gold-rimmed plates lined the back of the paper shelf and a vase of pink roses enhanced the effect of the floral-trimmed china. The whole thing was Victorian-friendly, ultrafeminine and way too pink. "Whoa. Girly. Where are the soccer balls? Baseball gloves. You don't really like this, do you?"

Meredith's gaze cooled like hot maple syrup on fresh snow, but Cam kept his eyes on Rachel. She made a pretty fair imitation of his frown and shook her head. "Way too prissy. Please."

"Well, I like it," Meredith announced. "It would be beautiful in a girl's room over a pink-sprigged floral print with white upper walls."

Cam pretended to gag. "You're kidding, right?"

"Not in the least." She sent Rachel a soft smile. "There's nothing wrong with being a tomboy who enjoys pretty things."

Meredith's words reinspired Rachel's sparkle. Cam thought of her bedroom at home. He'd painted it ivory when they moved into the old place a couple of years ago. Work and parenting had kept him from making the changes he'd envisioned when he bought the small farm, but the girls didn't seem to care. Life kept them plenty busy. Who had time to notice things like room color? Wallpaper? Please.

Rachel's profile said otherwise, reason enough right there to limit her time with Meredith. He'd worked hard to raise the girls to be strong and independent. Assertive and athletic. All too soon maturing hormones would thrust them into a new world of girliness, but Cam refused to rush that process. His motto: All A's, No B's. Athletics and academics, no boys allowed. At least until the girls were thirty or so. Then they'd talk.

"Gotta go get your sister, kid."

"Okay." Rachel nodded and smiled, but Cam noticed the smile didn't reach her eyes, eyes that drifted back to the feminine border.

He ignored the longing look and faced Meredith. "This afternoon good for you? Around two?"

"Fine." She didn't smile at him, but squatted low to share a smile with his daughter. "Thanks for the advice. I like the way you see colors."

Rachel's warm expression said the words meant more than just a casual compliment. "Thank you. I liked working with you."

"Then we'll have to do it again," Meredith promised. "Since your dad and I will be working together, that shouldn't be a problem."

She stood and Cam noticed the same wince he'd witnessed in the mercantile, as if her knees didn't care to cooperate.

He had a couple of joints like that, but the fact that Meredith didn't acknowledge it this time scored extra points in his book. Not that he was keeping score. And the cool look she sent him said she wouldn't care if he was keeping score because he'd gone into the minus column for not jumping on the teacup-and-flower bandwagon.

Oh, well.

Raising girls in a world rife with sensuality and innuendo was difficult enough for a man alone. Feeding into girly mumbo jumbo didn't make sense to him, especially for two gifted competitors like Sophie and Rachel. No, he'd stick to the familiar basics. Home. Work. Family. And sports channels on cable.

He jerked his head toward the mélange of wall-covering books in front of Meredith. "We'll discuss this—" he made a face to underscore his negative opinion of wallpaper "—later, okay?"

"Which ones to use? Perfect." She sent him a pert smile, a quick flash of teeth that said she'd go toe to toe with him. A long time ago, he'd have enjoyed that prospect. Now?

Not so much.

Meredith called her sister-in-law Callie once Cam left the store. When Callie answered with a quick hello, Meredith waded in. "Explain to me again why men are necessary?"

"Propagation of the species?"

"Modern technology could argue otherwise."

"Because they're better at digging up septic tanks and killing spiders?"

"There are machines for the first, and I can squash a spider with barely a grimace."

"Because they smell good on Sunday morning?"

Meredith had been close enough to Cam to know he smelled good on Saturday mornings, too. Very good, in fact, a hint of savory and spice. She hauled in a breath and asked for the third time that week, "Refresh me on why you and Matt are too busy to fix up this old house for me."

"Cam can't do it?" Callie asked. Meredith's moment of silence offered answer enough. "Oh, I see. Cam *can* do it and you're running scared."

"Annoyed possibly. Not scared."

"And he hasn't had an easy time since losing his wife," Callie continued.

"A fact everyone left out of the equation," Meredith muttered. "Why didn't someone tell me he was a widower? With kids?"

Callie hesitated.

Meredith read the conversational gap and sighed. "All right, I get it. I'm not exactly approachable about the past, all the teen drama."

"Those were rough times for you and your family." Callie's voice held assurance and affection. "I saw that in Matt. I see it in you and Jeff. When parents mess you over big time, it's an adjustment that can take a long time to fix."

Meredith didn't want or need fixing. She was hardworking and industrious, with great shoes and hair. Although her nails could use some work, she noted, looking down. And when did looking good become a crime?

"Mere, we'd do it if we could." Callie's tone softened and Meredith felt like a first-class jerk for playing the guilt card. "You know that."

Meredith did know that, but changing family dynamics fast-forwarded her into a new reality. Callie and Matt were expecting a baby and Matt was in the process of adopting Callie's son, Jake, an eight-year-old sweetheart.

Meredith's older brother Jeff had gotten married on New Year's Eve, and if Hannah's recent pale features were any indication, Meredith figured she'd have two new family members before year's end. Two bundles of joy to feed and rock. Anticipation mixed with envy. There was a time she'd thought of her future in those terms. Home. Family. Cute husband. Children.

An incoming text interrupted her pity party. She saw three words and Cam's number, and smiled in spite of herself while Callie was left hanging.

Pink teapots? Really?

The shared joke jerked her out of her self-imposed funk. "I'll talk to you later, Callie. And give Jake a hug for me."

"Will do."

Meredith saved Cam's text, put the phone away and closed the wallpaper books. Once outside, she drew a breath as frigid March winds swirled dust devils of stinging snow mixed with rain beneath her coat. Warmth came late in the foothills. She'd grown accustomed to softer springs in Maryland. Early buds, cherry blossoms, spring bulbs burgeoning forth. That wouldn't happen for a while in the Southern Tier of New York, but lamenting the weather didn't make the short list. Weather was what it was.

Great hair? Meredith walked by the old-time mercantile, shoulders back and head high, just in case Claire Dennehy was watching.

Great hair was priceless.

Chapter Four

"I can't find Sally."

"What?" Cam set aside the wood specs he'd been configuring, closed the laptop and slipped it into the cushioned bag that afternoon.

"Sally, the kitten. She's gone."

"You named that last kitten? Even though she's not staying?"

"Well, she still needs a name," Rachel interjected practically as she burrowed into her coat like a pup chasing its tail. "All little kitties need names, Daddy."

Sophie followed them to the car, her reluctance to leave slowing her step, shading her gaze.

"The mom will find her, honey. They always do."

Sophie looked up at him, pensive, then shifted a troubled look to the barn. "Are you sure? She's awfully small. And the other two are right there with their mom, eating."

"I'm sure."

"Daddy, can we play dress-up at Meredith's?" Rachel's concern was more readily appeased than Sophie's. Today was no exception.

"You mean Miss Brennan's?"

"She doesn't care. Really." Rachel gave that notion a dismissive wave and grasped his hand. "I think she likes us, Daddy. And it would be fun to dress up in old-fashioned clothes in her house."

"Of course she likes you," Cam told her. He ruffled her hair as she climbed into the car, then winked at Sophie on the other side. "You're the best girls ever. But we don't have any old-fashioned stuff."

"I know." Rachel frowned, attempting to reason this out. "We could get some. I wonder where you buy them?"

Cam didn't have a clue. "I don't think you do. I think people, like…leave them to you."

"Huh?"

"You know, like old people in your family."

"Like Grandma?"

The unlikelihood of that came through Rachel's tone and showed on her face.

"Not everybody keeps that kind of stuff," Cam explained.

"Well, they wear old-fashioned things in the parade every year," Sophie offered as she buckled her shoulder belt. "Somebody must know where to get them."

"Do we care that much?" Cam settled his laptop bag on the front passenger seat and met the girls' gazes through the rear-view mirror once he'd taken his seat. "Because I can check it out if we do."

Sophie looked tempted but stayed quiet. Rachel nodded as she clipped her seat belt. "Yeah. It would be great. And I think Meredith would like it. She likes having us around."

Good thing, thought Cam, *since we're going to be underfoot the next few months.* He double-checked his tool list, then started the engine. "But remember, this is a job. You need to be good while I'm working or I have to find a sitter for you."

He didn't miss their exchanged glances. "Not Grandma, right?" Sophie made a face that inspired Rachel's giggle.

Grandma didn't make Cam's short list of options, either,

but he wasn't a fan of disrespect. "Your grandmother loves you. She's just got her own way of doing things."

"Yeah. Mean."

"Rachel."

"Sor-ry."

She stretched out the word as if underscoring her sincerity, but Cam knew better. Rachel called things as she saw them, but he didn't want to raise mouthy kids. "You guys have your books?"

Sophie patted her backpack.

Rachel looked guilty.

Cam held up three books about an irascible kindergartner whose antics charmed kids of all ages and handed them over the seat. "Luckily, one of us was paying attention."

She grinned. "Thanks, Daddy."

"You're welcome. And I've got snacks packed, but don't mess up Miss Brennan's house, okay? Or leave food crumbs around for the mice."

"Real mice?"

"Or rats?" Sophie wondered, intrigued. "Will you pay us if we catch one?"

Cam hesitated, then nodded, unsure how Meredith would handle that idea. Rodents were a fact of life in the country and he paid the girls fifty cents for every mouse they caught, inside and outside. He paid a dollar for rats, but they'd only bagged two of those over the past few years, thanks to Dora, their white-backed calico cat. Dora hunted regularly, as evidenced by the furry gifts she left on their side porch.

She'd had three kittens a few weeks back, two of which were promised to friends.

Kristy had loved kittens. Cats hadn't been allowed in their apartment, but he'd promised they'd get one once they had their own place. She didn't live long enough for that promise to become reality.

His fault.

Guilt festered, an angry wound in need of cleansing. But there was little to do for a wounded man who left his wife to die on the couch.

Pneumonia, the doctor said.

Five years later, Cam still felt a slap of disbelief that people died from pneumonia in this day and age, especially young women like his wife. But he *should* have known because he knew her lungs had been compromised as a child. He'd watched her use an atomizer for exercise-induced asthma. Problems in her first year had taken her to the hospital several times with infant pneumonia. What he hadn't known was that the effects of those early problems could prove dangerous to the twenty-seven-year-old woman that shared his love, his life, his bed.

"What's wrong, Daddy?"

He flicked a glance toward Rachel, erased his concerns and shrugged. "Nothing, honey. I'm just pondering how to do things at Miss Brennan's."

"Oh." Rachel nodded, accepting, then sighed. "I love her hair. Don't you, Sophie?"

Sophie darted a glance between Rachel and her father. Cam caught the tail end of the surreptitious look while paused at a stop light. "It's all right," she answered, purposely nonchalant.

"It's gorgeous." Rachel laced her observation with full drawn-out emotion. "I want hair like that when I get bigger."

"I don't."

Rachel eyed her sister and shrugged. "Well, you couldn't have it anyway. You've got dark hair. And it's straight. I've got curls like Meredith."

Cam cringed. The girls barely knew Meredith and already they were arguing about hair. What was next? Nails? Makeup? Boyfriends? "God made you different because you are different, Rach. That doesn't make curls better than straight or vice versa."

"Vice-a-whatta?"

"It doesn't matter what your hair looks like," he pressed.

Sophie's eye roll said otherwise.

Rachel just laughed. "Of course it does. It's hair. It's supposed to look nice. Don't you like the way Meredith's hair looks, Daddy? All shiny and soft?"

Do not go there.

"How we act is more important," Cam explained, feeling defensive and out of the loop, "than how we look outside."

Sophie stayed quiet, staring out the window, then leaned forward. "You get your hair cut all the time, Daddy."

"Yes." He drew the word out, wondering. "I have to look decent to teach."

"What if we want to look nice, too?"

Where Rachel finagled, Sophie calmly reasoned. Her words stabbed Cam. Could they possibly think they didn't look nice? They were beautiful, lovely, adorable girls. They didn't need artificial enhancements to make that more noticeable. He paused at a stop sign and met Sophie's honest look.

"You always look nice, honey."

She stayed silent, their gazes locked. Cam glimpsed a hint of the woman she was to become when she sat back and resumed gazing out the window, her face and posture quietly shutting him out.

He'd blown it, big time, but he had no idea why. Or how. Or why hair mattered to a pair of little girls who should be more interested in crushing opponents on a soccer field than playing with dolls.

As he turned into Meredith's driveway, his mother's warning resurfaced. He'd worked hard to raise grounded, gracious girls. Two days after meeting Meredith, he felt like Commander Queeg, murmurs of mutiny surfacing around him.

He parked near the side door and started to unload his gear. For the next few months he'd be here in whatever spare time he could muster. But the girls...

His precious girls.

He'd worked hard to direct them to things of import. If being around Meredith elevated looks and fashion higher than they should be, he'd seek another option. Yes, he needed the money this job would bring. He'd called the orthodontist's office and set up Sophie's first appointment to get the ball rolling.

But no amount of money could coerce him to risk his daughters' emotional well-being. He'd recognized that early on, and refused to leave them with his mother more than occasionally for that very reason. Her negativity could quash their ingenuity, and he wouldn't have that.

But he wasn't about to go the other way, either, and have them turn into prima donnas, more concerned with appearance than content.

As the girls rushed the side door with their book bags in hand, Cam sent a look skyward. If only he'd been more on top of things five years ago, Kristy would be here, taking care of the girls, teaching them soccer drills and playing house with them. But she wasn't, and there was only one person to blame for that, the husband who'd promised to love and cherish her, in sickness and in health.

He'd blown that big time with his wife. He had no intention of risking a grievous mistake with his daughters.

The bang of the side door preceded the hurried sound of small, running feet. Meredith grinned in anticipation, rose, rolled her shoulders to loosen them, then put a choke hold on an emotional upsurge when Cam's cautioning voice followed the rapid footsteps.

"Girls. No running. This is a house, not a soccer field. Meredith?"

"I'm here." She descended the wide, turning staircase quickly, feeling his upturned gaze, pretty sure the inside temperature had risen indiscriminately with his arrival. Or maybe it was her personal internal temperature, in which case a nice, cold glass of tea should do the trick.

One look into Cam's sky-blue eyes said tea wouldn't cut it.

Meredith hid that realization behind a mask of calm, a look she'd perfected while dealing with pretentious spa customers who thought money more valuable than good manners.

She wouldn't have that problem in Wellsville and Jamison. Here she'd have to deal with the naysayers who thought great haircuts, pedicures and facials were acts of self-indulgence.

Meredith knew better. She'd watched her father ruin his life and his health by poisoning his system with drugs and alcohol.

Taking care of one's self was a reverent act. God offered one body, one life. Meredith believed that. And while painted nails might not provide world peace, didn't it make sense to add to the beauty of the world, not detract from it?

Cam would probably laugh at her assertion, but he'd be wrong. Looking nice fed heart and soul, and a good spa should be a peaceful, joyous experience. No matter what her fine carpenter thought of the whole deal. "You wanted to check upstairs?"

"Yes." He thrust his chin toward the back porch. "I brought my tools along. I'm going to lock them inside the kitchen if that's all right with you. The back porch locks, but the windows make the tools pretty noticeable, and it's harder to break in through two rooms."

"Has that been a problem around here?" Meredith couldn't imagine it, but...

"Yes," Cam admitted. "There have been a bunch of things gone missing from people's cars, garages, porches. Saleable stuff, and my tools would bring a nice price to a thief. And most of them are portable."

Meredith moved toward the porch. "Let's bring them inside now, then. That way it's done when we're tired later."

"We're?"

Okay, she'd had it with that little note in Cam's voice that doubted her abilities to walk and chew gum at the same time. She pivoted. "If you've got something to say, Cameron, say it now. Get it off your chest, and let's deal with it, because I haven't spent the last fourteen years working night and day to come back here and have you dismiss my work. First of all—" she waggled a finger while he took a wise half step back "—we were kids, it was a long time ago, and things didn't work out for a wide spectrum of reasons, so if that's what's bothering you, I suggest you drop it. It's over. Done. Finished. And second…"

She leaned in, narrowed her gaze and wished she'd kept her heels on. Without them he had a distinct height advantage, and that brought her face-to-face with a strong, broad chest. Nevertheless… "Taking care of your body, your skin, your face and your hair isn't a bad thing. It's food for the heart and soul, and—" she held up two fingers this time, pressing her point "—statistics prove that while women could generally care less about a man's aging, a hint of gray, laugh lines, a thickening middle—"

He sucked in a nonexistent gut, but Meredith refused to laugh. They'd have this out here and now if they were going to be able to work together at all. "Men tend to flock toward younger women. So if looking good keeps a man from looking elsewhere, I don't think that's a bad thing."

"Decent men don't look elsewhere, Mere."

The softness in his voice said he sensed dangerous ground and would tread softly, while his words rang true. But Meredith had been surrounded by financially comfortable men with less than stellar virtue, starting with her father and ending with the man she'd thought she known. Loved. Trusted. Experience had shown her that a fair number of successful men thought nothing of breaking vows. Or lying and schmoozing to get what they wanted.

"While that's true, there's still nothing wrong with men

or women wanting to take care of the vessel God gave them. Their body." She stepped back and gave a wave in his general direction. "If looking good isn't wrong for you, then why is it wrong for me? For women?"

His expression changed. Deepened. For a quick take of breath he looked thoughtful, but then he latched on to one thing of note, arched a brow and sent her a teasing smile. "I look good?"

He looked better than good, but she was *not* going there. "I meant it as an example."

"For teaching purposes only?" He moved a step closer, and yes, he *did* still smell good, making her wonder if he'd reapplied the scent because he knew they'd be seeing each other, or if he managed to smell good all day without reapplication, a thought that made her want to draw closer. Just to see.

She didn't.

But he did, and it was impossible to miss the glint in those blue eyes, a twinkle that said…

She had no idea what it said, but the sparkle drew her and she had no intention of being drawn to a guy who thought her simply decorative.

She started to turn, but he caught her hand as naturally as he had all those years before. His fingers melded with hers, the skin tough and calloused, firm and solid. Pinpricks of awareness clenched her gut. He drew closer, held her gaze and made a face of regret. "I apologize for being a jerk."

She started to shrug him off, pretending it didn't matter, but he moved closer and tipped her chin up, a move she remembered well. "It was rude. I can admit I had preconceived notions about all this." He waved his free hand around the gracious old house. "You've set me straight. I promise to keep an open mind. Generally."

She growled.

He grinned and released her hand, and she was pretty sure

a fairly good piece of her heart. But she'd learned the hard way that men were not always what they seemed.

Was that true with Cam?

Probably not, but Meredith wasn't in a position to take chances. She'd lost her job, and probably a good share of her credibility by believing the wrong guy. She'd smartened up, but couldn't afford more mistakes.

She'd been fooled once.

Her fault for being naive.

Letting herself get fooled twice?

Not about to happen, and definitely not in her hometown where private moments were a backyard conversation away from being common knowledge.

She led the way to the porch and helped lug Cam's tools into the kitchen. She'd do whatever it took to guard Cam's stuff.

She'd do even more to protect her heart.

Chapter Five

You can do this.

Eyeing the short walkway linking her car and Heather's entry, Meredith wasn't so sure.

She approached the door of the somewhat worn Federal-style building in Wellsville, noted the Closed Mondays sign, and hesitated.

A part of her wanted to run.

Another fraction longed to turn back the hands of time and fix things, an impossible task made harder by a guilt span of fourteen years. She raised her hand to knock, but a voice hailed her from above. "It's open, Mere."

She stepped out from under the overhang and looked up. "Hey, Heather."

Heather Madigan jerked a thumb. "Come on in. Coffee's fresh."

Her voice and easy acceptance made Meredith feel more like a jerk, deservedly. As she let herself in, the door emitted an old, familiar squeak, a welcome whine that reminded customers of where they were.

"Same door," she noted as Heather hurried into the room. Heather had gained weight, something she'd struggled with all through high school, but the look of cautious question in her face, her eyes, said Mere's visit was only a little surprising.

Heather waved a hand toward the door and motioned left toward the kitchen. "I could change it, but it was always that way when Mom was running the shop. It reminds me of her."

"Your mother was a good woman," Meredith said softly. She faltered, then frowned in apology. "I'm sorry I didn't come back for her service. Her funeral. It was rude."

"Everybody gets busy, Mere." Heather poured two mugs of coffee, grabbed out milk and sugar, then turned. "It's understandable."

"It wasn't that." Meredith figured if she was going to wipe the slate clean, best to do it now. "I just couldn't face coming home then. Seeing people. Having them talk."

Heather settled a look on her that mixed common sense and compassion. "You always cared too much about that. You worried Mama something fierce because she said you'd fall head over heels for the first guy with a good line that came your way because you wanted desperately to be loved."

The truth in Sandy Madigan's words must have shown in Meredith's face because Heather stepped forward. "And that's what happened, right?"

Meredith hadn't come here to spill secrets, but Heather's look of sympathy touched old feelings, rusty from disuse. "Let's just say your mother's common sense held true. Like always." Meredith walked back to the doorway separating the salon room from the small kitchen. "It looks the same."

Heather frowned. "I'm not sure that's a compliment."

"It is." Meredith turned her way and inhaled. "The same scents, too. Coffee, shampoo, neutralizer."

Heather laughed. "Brady hated that smell. He complained loud and long about how he smelled it in his shirts. In his food. How he couldn't even go upstairs to get away from it."

"So he left." Meredith set the words out gently. To her surprise, Heather didn't look all that disturbed.

"He never meant to stay, Mere. I was the one pushing, always. For a ring, then a wedding, then a family. He didn't want any of it, but I was too young and naive to see that. Or admit it to myself."

"How's Rory?"

Heather's smile broadened. "Amazing. So sweet. So smart. She'll do more than this someday." She spread her arms wide, indicating her attached-to-the-salon home. "I'll make sure of it."

Meredith pondered that comment, then pulled out a chair. "Can we talk?"

"Isn't that what we've been doing?" Heather supposed, but she pulled out the seat opposite and sat.

Meredith leaned forward and steepled her hands. "I'm starting a business."

Heather nodded.

"A spa."

A shadow darkened Heather's features as realization set in. A spa would go toe to toe with her business. "Where?"

"The Senator's Mansion."

"That's like three minutes from here."

"Yes." Meredith nodded, then slipped a proposal out of her bag. She extended it across the table to her old high school friend. "Here's the layout. The basic plan. Cam's doing the work for me." That news didn't shock Heather, because word spread fast in small towns. Maybe the following question would be a bigger surprise. A good one, Meredith hoped. Prayed. "And I was hoping you'd go into business with me. Be my partner."

Heather's eyes shot up. "What?"

Meredith hesitated, with good reason. She'd stomped the dust from her hometown off her feet fourteen years past and hadn't looked back, not even as much as a Christmas card to her old friend.

Talk about cold. Stupid and unfeeling.

Now she had a chance to right old wrongs. Isn't that what Matt had intimated? That she needed to make amends where needed? And wasn't that what Christ instructed the throngs that gathered to hear him speak? To forgive, go forth and sin no more.

Heather was the perfect starting point. "I've got a great head for business, for spa procedures, for running a large-scale shop. What I don't have is customers."

Her admission softened Heather's look of surprise. "I've got plenty of those."

"And it would be a good pairing." Meredith leaned in farther. "You and I always worked well together. We learned at your mother's feet, we go-fered until we were old enough and pesky enough to do nails. Then hair. And I've worked with a lot of stylists over the years, but no one better than Sandra Dee Madigan."

Heather put her head in her hands, groaned, then grinned. "That name. So funny. But so endearing."

"She was a great lady."

"I know. I miss her so much." Heather glanced around, misty-eyed, then reached for a tissue. "I keep these everywhere," she confessed. "Women get to talking and then they spill their guts about everything, and we have a cry fest, and go through crazy boxes of tissues."

Meredith considered that. "That part is different with a spa. People aren't so close together. There's more autonomy."

"Is that good or bad?" Heather wondered.

Meredith made a face. "Until just now I considered it the norm, but you've given me reason to rethink part of the layout. Because I think people would miss this." She nodded toward the closer, tighter spacing of the old-style salon. "And we don't want that."

"I don't have a lot of money, Mere." Heather faced her, square and honest. "I had to re-mortgage when Brady took off and there's no leverage to do that again."

"We've got start-up costs from Gram," Meredith explained. She opened the proposal to page four and pointed. "What you'd be bringing to the table is customers. Familiarity. A base from which to build."

Heather examined the papers, then sat back. "It's a lot to consider."

"Yes."

"I've done things my own way for a long time."

"And now there'd be two of us running things. And a crew to run."

"A crew." Heather's eyes sparkled. "I've always thought how fun it would be to run a place."

"And hard work," Meredith advised her. "You have to handle all the down stuff, the negative stuff, the backstabbing-girl stuff."

"Well, that won't happen, so that's not a problem," Heather declared.

"No?" Mere eyed her, amused. She knew better.

"No." Heather's voice took a more mature, not-on-my-watch air. "Not allowable. God offers people the opportunity to be kind or not. To be loving or not. There's nothing in the Bible that says I have to offer paychecks to jerks."

"There's not, but…"

"No buts." Heather met her gaze firmly. "If we're to do this, and I can't say I'm not totally tempted, you need to know I don't suffer brats well. You might want to think on that, Mere, because if we have stylists who can't get along, I'll pitch 'em to the curb. Life's too short and God doesn't expect us to reward misbehavior."

No-nonsense. Direct. Approachable. Honest.

Meredith had always loved those qualities in Heather. She'd forgotten how good that felt, to have a friend who didn't smoke-screen a conversation or blow sunshine at her right before they backstabbed her. She smiled, relieved. "I like the way you think."

"In this business, it's the only way to think," Heather advised.

It hadn't been that way in her old job. A percentage of that was her fault. She should have insisted on a neutral zone. Instead she'd worked zealously to put fires out, one after another, dealing with emotional tirades that had no place in a good business.

Live and learn.

She reached out a hand to Heather's. "No matter what you decide, I want you to know that I'm sorry for taking off like I did. Not coming back. Not writing or calling."

"You ran scared, Mere." Heather shrugged. "You hated your life here. Everyone knew that."

"I was young, but that doesn't excuse rudeness." Meredith stood and held Heather's gaze. "Whatever way this goes, I want you to know I'm real happy to be back. To see you."

"What's Cam's time frame on the work?"

Meredith smiled inside. Heather hadn't reacted to her news about Cam, but obviously she wasn't oblivious to the working arrangement. "July."

Heather angled her head. "That gives us three months." She raised her eyes to the salon room behind Meredith. "Come work here for the next few months. See if we can stand each other."

The offer was half humor, half challenge, but it made perfect sense. Meredith grinned. "Three days a week. That'll give me time to help with the changes at the spa. And if you're game, we can offer a hint of spa services. Get people in the proper mindset."

"I like it."

"Me, too."

Heather gripped her hand. "I'll see you tomorrow. 8:00 a.m."

"Then you can help me paint in the evenings," Meredith

added. "Bring Rory along. Cam's girls will be there when he's not running around."

Heather nodded. "And Rory's got Irish dancing lessons two nights a week, but it's just down the road so that's an easy drop-off and pickup."

Her words shifted bad memories to good ones. Step-toe practice. Rounds. Reels. Fun mop-of-curls wigs that she hadn't needed. Heather did.

"*Feis* weekends."

"Crazy fun." Heather's grin said she remembered them well. "But hard work, too. Although it kept me in shape."

Irish dancing provided amazing exercise. And strength training. Meredith moved toward the door, then turned back. "We could practice together. Now and again."

Heather made a face. "I'd look stupid. And old. Out of breath."

"We'd both look goofy, but only for the first few weeks."

Heather looked torn. "It's not like there's spare time," she argued.

"Making time to take care of our bodies is part of God's plan." Meredith tilted her head. "It would be fun and we'd feel good. And there'd be no stupid guys around like there are at the gyms."

"One of the very reasons I refuse to go there." Heather bit her cheek, then shrugged. "I've got nothing to lose but some time and twenty pounds that's on an upward trend."

"It's a deal." Mere grinned and opened the door. "I'll see you first thing in the morning...."

"And that will raise a few eyebrows."

Mere knew that. "And then you head over to the spa tomorrow night. We'll paint and dance."

A soft brightness seemed to lighten Heather's step. Ease her gaze. "I'll see you tomorrow."

Meredith walked back to her car, contemplating the interview. She'd taken a big step forward coming home. Assessing the locale. Finding a site, then buying it, but none of it compared with seeking out Heather and offering her a partnership, taking a firm step toward atonement.

Forgive us our trespasses, as we forgive those who trespass against us...

Heather had never done anything ill toward Meredith. Her humble home had been Meredith's saving grace, a niche of normalcy when chaos reigned in the Brennan family.

And when Meredith walked away, she'd never looked back, despite years of friendship. Faithfulness. Familiarity.

She made no attempt to excuse the sin, but she *could* try to make up for it. Be a better person than the one who'd left fourteen years before.

Jesus had told the labored, the weary, the uncomforted to come to Him, and He would give them rest. She wished she'd taken that gift to heart years ago, but she'd grown in understanding as wrongs piled up.

She would begin again, anew, washed clean in the here and now. And it felt wonderful.

"Hello, Earth to Mr. C. Is this the right angle for cutting this corner molding?"

Wake up, Cam. Put the Senator's Mansion and the beautiful woman out of mind while working. Easier said than done, and he hadn't even started the job at Meredith's yet. Uh-oh.

"Yes, Josh. That's perfect."

The teen nodded, braced his stance and made the cut, then examined the edge with a piece of fine sandpaper. The whine of power tools mixed with the smell of fresh-sawn wood, eight teens manning various work stations around the nearly complete home. Fine sawdust sprinkled the air. He and his class had rounded third and were heading toward home plate in the final year of a three-year project house off of Route 417. The World War I–style colonial had fallen on hard times when the family departed for a promised job in a Southern state. Left vacant, the home had suffered from lack of care until Cam's current state grant allowed the school to buy the property. Each day, groups of students were bused over. In a cooperative arrangement, Cam taught them the 1-2-3's of home repair, starting with basic demolition, then plumbing and electricity, before moving to wallboard. Hole repair. Finishing touches like installing windows and doors. Cabinetry. Life skills the kids would carry with them.

A movement caught his eye, and then his heart.

Meredith. Here. Now.

His eyes frowned from behind safety goggles.

His heart leaped.

He was glad Meredith could only see the first reaction. He moved across the living room of the house, pulled off his goggles and scowled. "What are you doing here?"

She didn't react to the scowl, which made him deepen it. "Looking for you."

"I'm working."

"I see that."

"You can't be here."

"Wrong-o." She held up a card from the administrative offices of the school. "As a taxpayer and a school sponsor and someone who is hiring you to work for me, I convinced the principal to give me a pass."

The principal, huh?

Cam would be sure to give Laura Henning a piece of his mind for sending Meredith over here. Of all the lamebrained...

He sighed, ran a hand through his hair, painfully aware of eight pairs of eyes watching while pretending to work. "Why are you here?"

"Partially to see your home-makeover project." Meredith waved a hand around. "I saw the photo spread in the online edition of the newspaper a few weeks back and I wanted to see it in person. This is magnificent, Cam." Her admiration for the classes' combined efforts sparked appreciation in the on-site kids' eyes.

Cam liked that. Some of the kids in his carpentry and construction classes didn't get a whole lot of positive reinforcement in their lives. Meredith's sincere approval uplifted them. He followed her into the kitchen work space, now complete. And beautiful.

"Wow. This is outstanding. Just...gorgeous," she finished, as if no other word would quite do.

She'd nailed the proper reaction to a job well done in a timely and cost-effective manner, two skills he believed in and taught well.

"Are the kids okay out there alone?"

He shook his head. "No. Which is why Laura shouldn't have sent you over. I've got to monitor them or nothing gets done."

"Sorry." She frowned, penitent, then moved his way. "I actually needed to ask you a couple of things and visiting your school project was a good excuse for that."

Cam withdrew his phone from a hip pocket and held it aloft. "See this? Great invention. Less intrusive."

"Do you answer it during the day?"

"Of course not."

"Then my way's better. I was filling out the paperwork for the zoning board's approval."

"Which means a vote," Cam interrupted. He frowned again. "I thought you had approvals all set?"

She shook her head. "Preliminaries, not final. But I need a few figures from you before I can submit the full application. I figured if I dropped this off, you might be able to get it done by tonight."

"Impossible."

She shrugged, accepting. "When you're able, then. They're meeting next Tuesday and my zoning petition requesting a change to a multiuse facility needs to be posted in the *Post-*

Herald. They said if I got the paperwork in by tomorrow afternoon, they'd put the notice in this week's edition and be able to discuss my application at next week's meeting. Maybe even vote the approval."

"On your first attempt?" Cam shifted a brow up. He was too familiar with small-town code. "Don't count on it. Are you pretty sure they're going to approve overall?"

She nodded. "According to them, it's a simple step up. While the building was used as a residence, it's zoned commercial so we've got the proper zoning. Now we just have to show a parking-to-patron ratio, the upgraded entrances and exits in case of emergency, upgraded electric, etc."

He didn't cover his reaction quickly enough because she stepped back, hands up, apologetic. "Listen, I know you're working here. I should have waited until tonight and dropped this off at your place, but I know the girls have practice."

"The Clarks are picking them up, then dropping them off at the mansion when practice is over. That way my time there isn't interrupted."

"Cam, thank you." She reached out a hand impulsively, her smile matching the quick move. "I didn't realize that, I figured you'd be running them around and that I wouldn't see you. I'll get out of your way now. Let you get back to work. But this…" she let her gaze roam the beautifully restored old-style kitchen jam-packed with modern amenities "…is just wonderful."

"Thank you." He followed her toward the front, then stopped her retreat with a hand to her arm. "Would you like the kids to show you what they've done?"

Meredith turned, surprised. Eight teens smiled as she redirected her attention their way. "I'd love it. You guys have time?"

"If the boss says so."

Cam hooked a thumb up. "Take her upstairs. Work your way down. I'll set up for tomorrow."

Meredith didn't hesitate, despite the high heels. High heels that showed off sweet ankles. Perfect calves. A skirt that hugged her body as if made for it, and considering Meredith's penchant for style, it probably had been.

He should have sighed in disapproval, but he was a normal man and there was nothing wrong with appreciating Meredith Brennan in well-fitted clothes.

She smelled like springtime, a mix of fresh air, sweet lilac and washed cotton hung on a line. How he'd managed to smell that over eight sweaty kids, power drills and saws, wood shavings and paint, well...

Obviously whatever she dabbed behind her ears did the job. And then some. He set out trim board for tomorrow's finishing touches, then moved to the stairs as they trouped back down, the whole group chattering like they'd found a new BFF.

"Amazing." She pivoted and stuck her hand out, shaking every kid's hand, making eye contact with each as she acknowledged them. "I wouldn't have believed this possible, how classes of students could work magic like this. I'd move into this house in a heartbeat."

"Really?"

"Oh, yes." She grinned at the girl who'd asked the question. "The bathroom remodel is gorgeous—I'd have plenty of room for all my hair stuff."

The girl laughed.

Cam and the boys groaned as one.

Meredith tipped Cam a smile that laughed at herself, and he felt his heart flutter once more, a sweet sensation of anticipation. Hope. It was a feeling he'd missed, but why was he feeling it now? With her? Because no way, no how, was he tempting fate by revisiting old mistakes.

Once burned, twice careful.

He cringed inside, his mother's negativity rising up. But he wasn't a starstruck teen anymore, a kid with open-ended options. He was a father, a teacher, a son, a home owner. He had responsibilities in their small community and he had no intention of forgetting that.

Although that smile tempted him to do just that. And that smell...

The kids dispersed back to their work stations. Meredith turned, stuck out her hand to him and clasped his firmly. "I'm sorry to have intruded, but—" she tipped her gaze beyond him to the smiling work crew "—I'm glad I did. You should be very proud of what you're doing here."

"I am," he admitted. What he didn't admit was how the clasp of her long, soft and sweet fingers in his had made him feel like he should keep them wrapped in his forever.

Whoa.

Cam dropped her hand like a hot potato, stepped back and shoved his hands into his back pockets. Tucked away they wouldn't be nearly so tempted to touch her. Hold her.

That ship had sailed a long time ago.

If Meredith suspected his feelings, she gave no sign and he breathed a sigh of relief as she headed out the door.

One of the boys chuckled and sent him a knowing look.

Cam scowled, but that just made all the kids add quiet asides, grinning.

Kids saw too much. But he'd have had to mark them down a grade if they *hadn't* noticed the electricity sparking between him and Meredith.

Worse? Cam enjoyed every minute of it. He contemplated the desk-size calendar mounted on the entry wall, with daily goals marking each square until the end of the term, mid-June.

Twelve weeks of working with Meredith, day by day.

He didn't stand a chance.

Chapter Six

"Meredith. How nice. Are you working here now?"

Meredith drew a breath before she turned.

Jacqui Crosby.

Jacqui's family lived opposite Claire Dennehy's home in Jamison. Both women had used the Brennan family as whipping posts back in the day. As if kids were void of hearing and emotion. Or was it petty jealousy because Meredith's family ran a successful business? Because they had money? Meredith knew firsthand that money offered little comfort to heartbreak. She'd tried to prepare herself for every possible circumstance that might rise up in Heather's salon. And compared to some of her regular customers along the Chesapeake Bay, Jacqui's brand of snark was ignorable. Almost.

Meredith flashed her a broad smile and a quick nod. "Heather took pity on me. Wasn't that nice of her?"

Heather rolled her eyes from behind Jacqui and added, "Coffee's fresh, Jacqui. And I've got bottled water, too."

"Coffee," declared the older woman whose roots should have been touched up weeks past. Why did so many bleached blondes find inches of dark-root growth acceptable?

Money, most likely. Spa procedures and salon upgrades got expensive, so keeping her costs under control was a must.

Meredith made a mental note that Allegany County had been roughed up economically until recently. Her prices needed to reflect that.

"Jacqui's doing a new growth touch-up and a trim today," Heather went on as she crossed the room. "Jacqui, how about if Meredith does yours and I'll take Lisa Grimm's cut and style when she comes in?"

"Lisa's on the schedule?" Meredith widened her smile. "I haven't seen her since I've been back. How's she doing?"

"Why don't you ask her yourself," Jacqui cut in smoothly, "while you do her hair? She's a simpler cut and Heather is accustomed to my style. I like my layers just so."

Ouch. Well. She'd just been put in her place by the town's younger version of Claire Dennehy. Great. But since it wasn't totally unexpected, Meredith let it slide.

"Sounds good to me." She turned and lifted a bunch of freshly folded towels. "Heather, do you want this whole pile next to the hair-washing sinks or shall I put some in the cupboard?"

Heather smiled, winked and nodded toward the small table. "There's fine. They're never in the cupboard long enough to stay so."

"Which means business is good." Meredith sent her an approving look and poured a cup of coffee. "And the coffee is delicious, as always. Although this won't help my caffeine addiction."

"And one should always be on the lookout for addictive behaviors." Jacqui flashed an innocent smile toward Meredith, as if she wasn't referring to Meredith's father.

"Unless it involves coffee or chocolate, I concur." Meredith met Jacqui's smile and matched it, determined to maintain an even demeanor. Even if it killed her, because killing Jacqui wasn't an option.

"Meredith!"

Lisa's welcoming voice broke the standoff. Meredith

turned into a really nice hug, a hug she hadn't known she needed until it happened. She returned the hug, laughing, then stepped back to look at Lisa's rounded belly. "How exciting! Congratulations!"

"It's marvelous."

Meredith reached out a hand to touch Lisa's expectant belly, then drew back. "Oops, sorry. May I?"

Lisa laughed out loud. "Yes. Everybody wants to touch my belly, it's the strangest thing."

"Baby connection," Heather added as she mixed the toner and developer for Jacqui's touch-up. "Babies draw people in. I think it reminds them of old times. Good memories. New life. Will this smell bother you, Lisa?"

Lisa started to shake her head, but Jacqui jumped in with her typical lack of finesse.

"I was sick nonstop with Brad." Jacqui's know-it-all tone shifted down. "And worse with his brother. So don't expect your next pregnancy to be problem-free."

Meredith was tempted to draw Jacqui's black plastic coloring cape up over her head, kind of like quieting a bird, but Lisa just leaned in and laughed. "Oh, Jacqui, I would not care. It took three years and some amazing science to get me to this point. I am blessed and I know it, and when those first bouts of morning sickness grabbed me, I welcomed them. My mama says a well-set baby makes its presence known."

"Your mama's right." Heather gave a firm nod as she measured, gaze down, intent on doing it once, doing it right. Meredith loved that about her.

Jacqui's face softened, just enough for Meredith to think there might be a nice person hiding within. But then she opened her mouth and Meredith realized it had been a trick of the light.

"Tell me that after you've gone through twenty-eight hours of hard labor. You'll be talking a different tune then, I expect."

Meredith stopped the train wreck of conversation by drawing Lisa toward the two shampoo sinks. "Come here, let me pamper you. When is this baby due?"

Lisa's look of gratitude empowered Meredith. "Six weeks."

"Oh, how lovely."

"Do you have kids, Mere?"

Meredith shook her head as she draped a cape around Lisa's shoulders, then waggled her fingers. "Single. Never married."

"The right guy hasn't come along, or career-driven?" Lisa arched a well-defined left brow as she settled back in the chair, her baby bump making her profile distinctive. And sweet.

"A little of both, I think." Meredith turned on the water, tested for temperature, then slowly wet Lisa's hair, watching the young mother's features relax as the warm stream bathed her head. "How about you? Who won your heart?"

Lisa's expression shifted slightly. "Joe Jackson."

"Really?" Meredith leaned down, surprised and delighted. "Oh, how cute will this baby be? With Joe's deeper skin tone and your hair, we've got a potential supermodel on our hands. Joe Jackson is a total hottie, Lisa."

Lisa's laugh erased the momentary shadow. "And he's the sweetest man on the planet. I couldn't ask for a better husband."

Meredith ignored the audible sniff that came from Jacqui's direction. Racially mixed marriages were common in the power belts of D.C., but here in northern Appalachia?

A little scarcer.

"What does Joe do?"

"He's a doctor. He joined the family practice run by old Doc Hayward, and he loves it."

"Good for him." Meredith finished conditioning Lisa's hair, then rinsed and toweled it gently. "And do we know if this is a boy or a girl?"

"A girl. Ava Marie."

"Love it!" Meredith gave Lisa a hand up. "That's the kind of name that grows with a child. Beautiful. Strong. Musical."

"Joe's mother's favorite hymn was 'Ave Maria.'" Lisa settled into the cutting chair with a small *oomph,* then rolled her eyes. "At least I still fit in the chair."

"Plenty of room," Meredith declared. She adjusted the chair setting and fingered Lisa's hair, assessing. "Did Joe's mother pass away?"

"Last year." Lisa shrugged, but her eyes said she missed the older woman. "She was a nurse, so she understood what we had to go through to get pregnant, and she was so supportive. So kind. So excited to be a grandmother."

"I'm sorry." Meredith met Lisa's gaze in the mirror and realized how blessed she was to still have her mother. Dana Brennan had stuck by her daughter through thick and thin, a strong, quiet woman of faith and fortitude. Would she be as supportive if she knew Meredith's past? Her foolish mistakes? Her prideful attitude that had pushed faith and morals aside?

Meredith didn't want to find out. Leaving the past buried worked best all around. She was back, she was invested, she was fine. Just fine.

"Well, I've got the distinct feeling that Jenny Jackson is watching us from above. Praying for us. Taking care of those babies that didn't make it this far."

Meredith's heart melted more. Lisa had clearly met adversity, but she hadn't quit. She'd forged ahead to make her dream of motherhood come true. "I will be praying for you and Joe. For this baby. How nice to be this beloved. Cherished. Wanted."

Lisa's eyes met hers in the silvered glass. Her gaze said she understood what Meredith didn't say, that she'd longed for a father who would love her. Care for her. Put her first, the way a father should.

It hadn't happened, but that was Neal Brennan's fault, Meredith realized. Not hers.

Cam loved his children that way. She saw it in his every action, weighing how his choices might affect his girls.

And she saw the same thing in Lisa's gaze, heard it in her voice. Children were gifts from God, a blessing, one and all. Recognizing that reaffirmed her decision to slip quietly away from Jude Anne's threats in Maryland. Dragging Sylvia Bellwater's children through the mud wasn't going to happen. Not on Meredith's watch, anyway. Keeping her tone light, she fingered Lisa's hair. "Short? Layered? Spiky? Pink?"

Lisa burst out laughing. "Layered. Easy. I want to be able to shower and let it dry while I take care of this baby. No fuss, no muss."

"You got it." Meredith lifted Lisa's hair, decided that spunky would suit her old classmate's elfin features, and got to work, chatting easily, catching up on fourteen years of news. And aside from the occasional clipped interjections from Jacqui Crosby's side of the room, it felt good.

"You're working for Heather?"

Cam didn't mean the words to come out so brusque and abrupt, but he'd been stewing on this for nearly three hours, questioning his estimate, wondering if he should have lowered the costs to spare Meredith some cash. His price was fair. He knew that.

But the idea that she was working in Heather's shop, then coming here and stripping old wallpaper, painting moldings, climbing ladders, sanding wall patch, well…

That seemed a little much, and he'd promised himself to never take a woman's efforts for granted again. And even though Meredith's presence was strictly business, a man's God-given responsibility was to look after women like Christ loved the church.

He'd failed miserably before.

He was smarter now.

One glance into her questioning and possibly insulted eyes said he might be off-target. So maybe *not* smarter.

Great.

"I'm working with Heather, yes. It makes sense to establish a client base, to get to know people again. And Heather's always been easy to work with."

"So you're trying to steal her customers?" Cam stared straight at her, trying to make sense of this and failing. "How is that a good thing?"

Meredith shifted her gaze away, but not before he recognized the shadow of hurt he'd put there. "I don't steal, Cam. Heather's thinking about coming into business with me here. In fact she'll be here soon to help paint this trim."

"A partner?"

Meredith nodded, but didn't look up, probably thinking he was the biggest jerk in the world for drawing quick assumptions. "Yes. I've got the financial backing from Grandpa's estate and Grandma's loan. Heather's got the client base. Working together makes a whole lot more sense than putting a friend out of business, right?"

"Most people don't take fourteen-year breaks from friendship and come back expecting everything to be as it was."

"Am I doing that?" She raised her gaze to his and the look in her eyes made him feel like a louse. "I hope not. I'm just trying to start over. There's no law against that, Cam."

There wasn't. But he wasn't about to forget how quickly she'd taken off the last time, without even a backward glance.

Nope, Meredith was good at looking out for Meredith. He'd found that out a long time ago. But they'd both moved on. And then come back, full circle.

Scary thought. And the fact that she looked real good in paint-speckled sweats and a long-sleeved T-shirt meant that she just plain looked good. Why was he noticing that?

She flashed him a look of question. "Are the girls at soccer practice?"

He nodded, glad for the change of topic. "Yes. They'll get dropped off here around eight."

"Have they had supper yet?"

He tried to read censure in the question, but couldn't. He shook his head. "We eat late on soccer nights. Hard to run around on a full stomach."

"Pizza good?"

Cam frowned. "Pizza's always good, but…"

"I was just thinking that Heather will be here, Rory's coming after her Irish dancing lesson, and if you and the girls are here, it makes sense to grab something, right? Because it's late by then."

"I can give them mac and cheese at home. Or sandwiches. We're used to this."

"Okay."

He was glad she gave up easily. Bad enough he was depending on friends and other team parents to run his girls around, but to be spoon-fed supper?

Not about to happen.

He headed to the first floor, and waved to Heather when she came in a short time later. Meredith wanted six bays tucked into the L-shaped corner.

Did she really think they'd have six customers at once? Wouldn't it be smarter to start with three or four and add as business grew?

But she'd been firm, so six it was.

And then a coloring station, centered, with the hair-washing sinks. Like they couldn't do that in the regular barber's chairs?

Not in a spa, she'd told him.

He measured, assessed, marked and drew a rough sketch, then went to his computer, opened his computer-aided design program and let the software do the work it would have taken days to complete fourteen years ago.

Sweet.

"That's amazing."

Meredith's voice spiked neck hairs he'd forgotten he had. Or was it the soft feather of her breath against his collar, his skin? He pulled left, then turned his head.

Big mistake. Huge. Her soft skin had a peppering of sawdust on her left cheek, just enough to make him reach up. Brush it away.

She turned into the touch and that one little move brought back a host of memories. Good times. Sweet times. Teenage romance.

But thirtysomethings weren't allowed to wallow in emotion. They were grown-ups, with jobs to do. He stepped back, breathed easier, and nodded toward her cheek. "Sawdust."

She smiled.

He felt his heart slip back in time, and this time it was harder to draw it up and out, but he managed. With concerted effort.

"This program does the cabinetry work for you?"

"The layout, cuts and design. I still get to run the saw."

Her smile of appreciation widened. "Computers only go so far. Still, it's remarkable, isn't it?"

"Yes."

She shifted her gaze to his and they both knew he wasn't talking about the computer software anymore. Not when she was this close and smelled this good. Not when he'd just brushed dust from her face and longed to cradle that cheek in his hand. Feel her skin again. Hear her sigh.

She stepped back first. "You and I will be working on separate floors during this project."

He didn't pretend to misunderstand her edict. "You're right. Why take a chance on messing things up?"

She bristled.

He laughed.

The girls stormed in, kicking off soccer cleats in the outside entry, and dumping their bags alongside. "Dad!"

"Meredith!"

It was funny, to hear them shout out to Mere the same way they did to him. And sweet.

Not to mention downright frightening. No way was he about to let his girls fall in love with Meredith Brennan and her perfect-hair-and-nails manner. Although right now her hair was way less than perfect, her nails were chipped, and she looked…

Wonderful.

He swallowed hard, grabbed the girls in a hug, glanced at his watch and said, "Gotta go, girls. School tomorrow."

"Aw, Dad."

"Can't we stay, just a little? Our homework's done."

"Just fifteen minutes, Dad? Please?"

He wanted to say no. He needed to say no. They had to get home, shower, eat and get to bed.

So why did the word *yes* fall from his lips like it was meant to be there? Was it the little look of entreaty Meredith sent him? That sheen of hope in her eyes?

She was getting to him. She knew it. He knew it. But they were adults and professionals. They could handle this. Right?

"Girls." She grabbed both their hands and tugged Sophie and Rachel toward the wide staircase. "Come see what I'm doing in your room."

"They don't have a room," Cam called after her, but he knew it was useless. Not one of them had the decency to afford him even an over-the-shoulder glance. They just barreled up the stairs like long-lost friends and disappeared in a flurry of footsteps and giggles.

It felt kind of good, actually. But he couldn't let it feel good, he couldn't risk his girls' hearts.

Or his own, for that matter.

But snatches of laughter floated down the stairs, and when a student of his showed up with a sheet pizza a few minutes later, Cam realized he'd been duped.

No way could he get those girls out of here, past the good-smelling food, and not feed them. And since his own stomach was happy-dancing a jig of anticipation, he couldn't blame them. "Mere? Pizza's here."

"Perfect. We'll be right there."

She slipped him a twenty when they came down the stairs. He started to protest, but she pushed the bill into his hand and held it there, which meant he had to pretend having her hold his hand wasn't totally delightful. "Feel free to buy me/us supper sometime, but this was my idea. Did you tip the guy?"

"Yes."

"Thank you." She smiled at him, hooked a thumb toward the kitchen, and added, "Girls, plates and paper towels are back there. And I put a table back there this morning, so we can actually sit while we eat."

"Awesome!" The normally quiet Sophie beamed and that heartfelt smile made Cam realize two things: one, that Sophie should smile more. And two, she smiled more around Meredith.

He was in big trouble.

Heather and Rory joined them from the back staircase, a narrow affair that led straight into the kitchen. Heather grabbed a diet soda, handed one to Rory and waved one in his direction. "Soda?"

He shook his head. "Water."

"Got it right here." Meredith slid a tall glass of water his way, then handed cups to the girls. "And milk for you ladies."

"I like root beer." Rachel piped the words in a hard-to-resist sweet voice.

Meredith flashed her a grin. "Me, too, kid. But tonight it's milk for strong teeth and bones. If you work hard all week, I might buy you a root beer milkshake at Meg Russo's ice-cream stand this weekend."

"Meg Romesser," Cam corrected.

"Well, she's about to deliver that baby, so it will most likely be Crystal or Jillian manning the ice-cream part of the business in any case," Heather added. "And she looks adorable."

"Does she?" Meredith's tone softened. Then the two women exchanged a look that meant nothing but trouble to unsuspecting men. Cam tipped his gaze down to the innocent-looking pair of girls he'd fathered.

"They start off all right," he drawled, then seized another piece of pizza with easy grace. "Little. Cute. Toothless. Kind of smelly."

"Hey!"

"Dad!"

He shot the girls a "gotcha" look of acknowledgment. "And then they turn into kids. Walking, talking, shoe-wearing, meat-eating kids."

Heather met his droll look and laughed as she nudged Rory's arm. "And they keep growing. Needing things."

"Shoes."

"Coats."

"Boots."

"School supplies."

"But we're cute," Rachel cut in, head tilted, looking like purity personified. "That's gotta count for something, right, Dad?"

"You're all right." His smile of approval said more and she preened under the light banter. Her actions made him realize that he didn't tease and laugh with them as often as he could. He'd have to concentrate his efforts more. Relax a little. Breathe.

But when bills mounted and time grew short, everything got set on automatic.

"Well, I don't know much, being an old spinster lady." Meredith settled into a chair alongside Sophie and shoulder-butted her gently. "But I think having two delightful girls would be something to crow about. When they're not fighting, that is."

Sophie sent her a guilty look.

Rachel just grinned.

Rory added, "That's the good thing about being an only child. No one to fight with but Mom."

"Thank heavens we don't do much of that," Heather said. "It's exhausting."

It was, Cam realized. When he had to bargain his way into and out of everything because the girls were so different, it tired him out. Made him feel wanting. A tiny light dawned, a hinted candle that said he didn't have to be all things to all people. His mother. Sophie. Rachel. There might be some days they'd just have to, well...deal.

"You know, kids are survivors." Meredith made the claim with no look of remorse or pathos. "And if parents do their best, that's all any kid can ask. Right?"

Her statement made it sound easy.

Raising kids alone was anything but.

And yet, the little flame of awareness flickered brighter. Stronger. Maybe he wasn't Dad of the Year, but he was pretty good. Right?

"I don't think God expects us to be perfect." Heather eyed a second piece of pizza, then took a distinct step back and didn't sigh. "But I do think he expects us to do the best we can with what we have. To inspire. To guide. To lead."

"With occasional trips to the woodshed," Cam added.

"Well, of course, that."

"Woodshed?" Sophie arched her delicate brows in question.

"What's that?" Rachel spoke around a ginormous bite.

He tapped her head lightly. "Manners."

She made a face but nodded, closed her mouth and chewed semi-politely.

"A woodshed is where you keep firewood." Meredith sent a point-blank look Cam's way, challenging him. "And that's all it is."

"We stack it by the barn," Sophie replied, matter-of-fact.

"But Dad never takes us there. We just go over there by ourselves."

Meredith met Cam's look across the table and something in the soft gaze of approval set his shoulders straighter. His chest firmer. "Your father loves you girls. But of course he wants you to behave."

"We know." Rachel finished her pizza, sighed, sat back and looked like she was about to fall asleep sitting right there, kitten-style. Cam was feeling mighty comfortable himself. Reason enough to stand up and get moving. Only, he didn't want to. Not really.

The grandfather clock in the front room chimed nine o'clock. Long past time for the girls to be home and tucked in. He stood, shrugged into his jacket and jerked his head left. "Girls. Let's move. Time for bed."

Rachel started to whine, but Meredith put a light hand to her shoulder. When the little girl turned, Meredith gave a gentle shake of her head. "Daddy gave you extra time already, right?"

"Yes."

Meredith smiled, not needing words to make her point. And then Rachel reached up to her, wanting the beautiful, stylish woman to hold her. And when Meredith drew the seven-year-old into her arms as if made for the job, Cam knew he was in deep, deep trouble.

Chapter Seven

She needed to stay away from Cameron Calhoun, and that's all there was to it.

Meredith swept mauve paint across a wide, carved porch-rail molding, then slowed her hand as she skated the wooden edge, wishing the detail work would distract her.

It didn't.

No, thoughts of Cam mentally replayed like an online video ad. The angle of his head. His thoughtful gaze. His art of self-examination, schooling himself in goodness. His hands, how they cradled wood and tile with a reverence she longed for, but she'd messed up on reverence a long time ago.

Her cell phone interrupted her roller-coaster thoughts. "Good morning."

"Mere, it's Mom."

Meredith grinned. Her mother was still getting used to caller ID, even though she had it on her cell phone. "I kinda figured that when your name and number came up in my screen."

"Of course." Dana Brennan's tone made light fun of herself. "Old habits die hard. Hey, listen, family dinner tomorrow night. Including Grandma."

"Ooh. Must be big news. Bet I can guess what it is," Meredith teased, laughing. "Between Hannah and Callie, the family's looking mighty green these days."

Dana laughed with her. "I know. These poor girls, God love 'em, it's a rough bunch of weeks, but what a joyous thing to celebrate. Babies. At last. After all this time. Are you free to be here?"

She and Heather were doing an Irish dance workout tonight and then she was working at Heather's salon tomorrow. "Wouldn't miss it. Do you need help with anything?"

"Did you suddenly become domestic?"

Meredith's smile broadened. "I can wash green beans. Or peas. Or something."

"You set up your business with that cute carpenter of yours and I'll cook, okay? Nothing wrong with focusing our time on our talents, darling, and yours isn't exactly in the kitchen."

So true. But… "He's not my carpenter, Mom. He's working for me."

"Uh, huh." Dana sounded unconvinced, which only meant she knew her daughter well. "Six o'clock good?"

"Perfect, Mom. Hey, can I bring a guest? No, wait—two guests?"

"Bring whoever you want," Dana told her firmly. "I'll make enough for an army and we'll toast these babies' futures."

"Excellent."

Meredith set the phone aside and fought the threatening surge of melancholy. She loved babies. She loved Callie and Hannah, her sisters-in-law. Of course she was happy for them. Ecstatic, even.

One fat tear dripped down her chin.

She wiped it away, frustrated by a stupid wave of thirty-something emotions.

She'd messed up, big time. She knew it, but few others did. If she'd been more careful, more faithful, more selective, she wouldn't have wasted over two years on Chas.

The thought bit deep, but she deserved the pain. She'd lived a life of carefree modern nonchalance until it came back to bite her, so she deserved the sting of reality. She'd given a key to her apartment to a married man. She'd given her heart and forgotten about her soul. She'd dallied with a lifestyle that seemed very contemporary and chic until she realized there was no tomorrow.

Yes, she'd been duped, but only because she allowed herself to be fooled. And the thought of his children, his wife... what the knowledge of their affair would do to them.

She'd lived that embarrassment as a child. No way could she do that to anyone else's children. And yet she'd put herself in a position to do just that.

Shame knifed her.

The phone rang again. Cam's number flashed in the small gray rectangle. Cam, who always chose the side of goodness and virtue. Cam, whose work showed dedication and devotion. Cam, whose daughters were lovely young ladies.

She stared at the ringing phone, then deliberately walked the other way. He'd leave her a message. That would be easier for her than hearing his voice, reading his pauses, wondering at his expression. She'd managed to taint her life, she knew that. She'd dealt with it and moved on.

But no way in this world was she about to stain his.

The steady *thump-thump-thump* drew Cam's attention that evening, but it was the reeling Celt pipes that pulled him up the broad staircase, curious. The sight of Meredith practicing some kind of jig or reel in the turret room stopped him cold.

Wild beauty surrounded her. Her hair had come free and followed her moves in waved abandon, her feet flying, arms still, chin raised, and her smile...

Oh, that smile.

She flashed it at Heather as they made a diagonal pass in opposite directions, a move he remembered like it was yesterday, not fourteen years ago. They'd danced en troupe and individually, she and Heather, and sometimes as a pair despite their physical differences, always vying for the number-one dance position while maintaining a strong friendship.

Until Meredith wiped the sleepy dust of Allegany County off her toe shoes and moved on without a backward glance.

Heather spotted him first. She gave a quick nod, missed a step, scowled and regrouped at the designated turn spot.

They spun, not quite in unison, but still pretty impressively for women who hadn't danced together in over a decade, then finished the dance perfectly, facing the curved bay of windows, each step timed to the music. When the fiddle sped up, then came to a quick halt, they stopped, feet in position, hands flat at their sides, smiles wide. As if they'd been doing it every day of their lives, only they hadn't.

An audience of one, Cam couldn't help himself. He clapped. He whistled, too, amazed how they felt the music and remembered the dance, the steps, the patterns, the moves.

Heather flashed him a grin of thanks.

Meredith looked like she'd just been blindsided, which she had. She hadn't seen him in the doorway; her part had kept her facing the opposite direction. His presence surprised her, and yet it shouldn't. He *was* working here.

"I'm grabbing a water," Heather announced. She slung a small towel around her neck and caught Meredith's eye. "Want one?"

"Yes. Please."

Heather offered Cam an "uh-oh" look as she went by, but Cam kept his face calm as he faced Meredith's frown.

"Why are you here?"

"I…work here." He elongated the words, drawing them out, making fun of her lightly.

"But you weren't going to be here tonight. You said so."

"I left my laptop last night because I was late with the

;irls. So tonight I dropped them off home and ran over here
o get it."

"They're alone?"

He nodded. "For ten minutes. Well." He glanced at his
ugged watch. "Fifteen. But that's a good way for them to
earn and earn independence. Fifteen minutes on their own
o prove that they're trustworthy."

"That's dangerous."

He shrugged. "Life comes with risk, and the girls know
heir routine. I'm trusting them to do it. They're not babies,
hey're seven and nine and what happens if they come home
omeday and the house is empty? Learning how to behave
n their own is a good step."

"But it's night. And dark."

"And the house is locked. And there are no bogeymen,
Mere."

Her expression said he was wrong about that, but he didn't
ave time to bore further. "Gotta go. I just heard the thumping
nd thought you might be jackhammering walls. Or some-
hing."

She made a face and didn't meet his gaze. "To Irish music?
Really?"

He shrugged. "I tune in the country station when I'm work-
ng. I like it. Makes me think more clearly."

"As you can see, the walls are intact."

He nodded and tried not to smile, but failed. "And you still
lance like a wild, Irish gypsy."

Her cheeks softened. Her eyes brightened, just for a mo-
nent; then the look dulled. Faded. "Irish gypsy, huh?" She
urned slightly, her profile taut. "That might explain a few
hings."

She stood stock-still, staring at the window beyond him.
Why?

He had no clue.

"You've got to leave."

He nodded, turned and headed for the stairs. "I'll see yo͏ tomorrow night."

"No."

He turned back, surprised. "Okay."

"My mother's having the crew over for supper. Wit͏ Grandma. I have to be there."

"It sounds nice, Mere. And the girls have soccer practic͏ until eight-thirty so I'll work here and then cut loose at eigh͏ and pick them up at the middle school."

"Okay."

"Okay."

He needed to get home. He'd left the girls on their own re͏ cognizance, and he knew they'd be fine, but his fifteen min͏ utes was stretching to twenty. He headed down the stairs a͏ a quick clip, then resisted the urge to see if she followed hi͏ progress with her eyes. Nope. It seemed as if his presenc͏ irritated her. Disturbed her. Just as well, really, because sh͏ was bothering the heck out of him.

She'd left the cookie basket in the just-delivered spa refrig͏ erator. Growling at herself for being obtuse, Meredith shove͏ the car into gear the next evening, headed north on Route 1͏ and turned back into the curving drive of the Senator's Man͏ sion wishing she'd paid closer attention to the clock.

She hadn't, and now she had to grab the cookie arrange͏ ment she'd picked up at the Colonial Cookie Kitchen and ge͏ to her mother's place on the south side of Wellsville withou͏ ruining dinner. She grabbed her cell, then paused her finge͏ over the number three, her mother's speed dial.

Two cars sat in the parking area adjacent to the future spa͏ Cam's and some sportin' hot red ragtop, spit-shined to refle͏ the late rays of the sun.

Who was here? With Cam?

Not your business.

She dialed her mother's number, then headed for the bac͏

door of the spa that led straight into the kitchen. No reason to disturb Cam's work or get herself all in a dither over what could have been and wouldn't be.

Been there. Done that. Not pretty.

She let herself into the kitchen just as Cam and a drop-dead-gorgeous natural blonde entered from the formal dining room slated to become the hair salon. With one touch of a button she disconnected from her mother. Some things a mother didn't need to hear.

"Mere."

"Cam." Meredith turned cool eyes to his right. Blonde. Beautiful. Young. Carefree.

Meredith decided she hated the petite woman on principle.

Cam jutted his chin toward the wall clock. "You're supposed to be at your mother's."

"On my way. I forgot these." She swung open the door to the refrigerator and pulled out a cookie arrangement slightly lighter than when she'd left that morning. "We've got mice."

Cam grinned, having no idea how close he was to possible annihilation if the blonde got any closer to his side. Or if she smiled any wider. Or...

Get a grip, Mere. He's not yours, she can't help her natural attributes, and you're not even supposed to be here. Let it go.

"The girls were here. And I tried calling you—"

She'd ignored his call an hour ago, knowing he'd leave a voice mail.

"And they were hungry so we nipped a few." He stepped forward, making the blonde appear more slim and petite than she already did.

Just another reason to dislike her.

Meow.

"I hope it's all right." Cam's gaze searched her face, wondering what was going on, why she'd be upset over a few cookies for the girls. And of course she wasn't upset about that, not a smidge.

The blonde, on the other hand?

Another matter entirely.

Cam stepped back as if suddenly realizing she was there. "Haley Jennings, meet Meredith Brennan. Meredith's the owner and developer of Stillwaters."

Meredith set the cookies on the table and extended a hand, claws retracted. For the moment. "Haley."

Haley grasped her hand like a long-lost friend, and that only made her seem nice and normal and more difficult to abhor, but if Meredith worked real hard, she'd find a way.

"This is beautiful," Haley announced. She swept the house a wave. "Great work, a marvelous eye for detail and balance, and what a clever and comforting idea, to use such a gracious piece of architecture for a wellness spa. I hope to be a regular customer, Meredith."

Meredith choked down a sigh. It was hard to stoke fires of animosity when the target spewed multiple complimentary things about your business venture. "Thank you, Haley. It's nice that Cam brought you by to see things."

Haley looked startled, then shook her head. "I kind of steamrolled him, actually. Left him little recourse."

Meredith arched a pseudo-sympathetic left brow in Cam's direction. "Poor baby."

Cam's smile almost got him kicked in the shins, but Haley saved him the pain.

"I'm converting the old furniture factory and showroom into a country-style street of shops called Bennington Station."

It took a moment for Meredith to follow this new train of thought. "The one at the interstate exit?"

"Yes, that's it." Haley waved a rolled-up sheaf of papers. "I'm having the preliminary work done by C and M Construction."

"My brother," Meredith cut in.

"Really?" Haley's smile broadened. "What an industri-

s family. Well, Matt and Hank are doing the rough-in con-
ruction for me, but there are parts that need to be finessed."

"And I've been told by many that Cam's the reigning king
finesse in Allegany County." Meredith rolled him a look
at he shrugged off.

"The timing's good." Cam indicated Haley's tube of plans
ith a jut of his chin. "By the time the standard carpentry
d utilities are in, I'll be done here and school will be out.
hat gives me nine weeks to take care of Miss Jennings' job."

"You're doing this yourself?" Meredith eyed the more pe-
te woman and tried to erase her tone of doubt.

Haley squared her shoulders. Her chin came up, very Reese
itherspoon, and while Meredith loved the actress's spunky
yle, she wasn't gung ho on having a prototype hanging on
am's every move, every word.

"I am. My great-grandfather was Wilt Bennington, the
an who started the Northern Appalachian Furniture Fac-
ry. And it was open for nearly sixty years, so definitely a
edit to his success. And then Grandpa had it, but by the time
came to his son-in-law, my father, the local economy had
ken a direct hit. My father did not have a head for business.
think running a factory and furniture showroom ranked
out dead last on his list of things to do, so it kind of died
f benign neglect."

Her words sparked a memory for Meredith. The old furni-
re factory hadn't just shut down. Part of it had been burned.
rson was suspected, but nothing had been proven. But she
membered that Haley's father had been targeted in the in-
estigation, and Meredith understood the repercussions of
uilt by association.

"Anyway—" Haley stuck out a hand to Cam and shook
is firmly "—you've got my cell number. If you could come
y and give me a ballpark estimate for the fine carpentry
ork, I'd appreciate it. I own the property and it's worth a
ir amount so I've got collateral for the bank's interest, but

I need these last two components on board to square up th
loan deal."

"I'll be there Saturday morning at eight," Cam promise

"Thanks." Haley flashed him a smile that showed pe
fectly even white teeth and Meredith decided then and the
to stop by the pharmacy and pick up teeth-whitening strip
Great hair should always be accompanied by a bright smil

Cam swung her way as Haley went through the back doo
his gaze appraising and more than a little amused. "Yo
thought she was with me."

"Did not."

The hinted amusement deepened. "Oh, you did. And
riled you, Mere."

"I'm not riled, I'm late. Big difference." She turned, de
termined to avoid his gaze, his smile, his teasing. Let hir
think what he would. She had places to go. Things to de
People to…

The kiss should have taken her by surprise, but it didn'
Not even close. It actually seemed like the long-lost welcom
home she'd been waiting for. Praying for. Longing for. Th
feel of Cam's mouth on hers, the way he wound his arm
around her, drawing her in, his embrace solid and comfor
ing. A part of her loosened, the knot of old hurts and pa
wrongs inside easing in the safety of Cam's arms.

"Oops." He broke the kiss eventually and dropped his fore
head to hers, his breathing sporadic and uneven. "I promise
myself I wouldn't do that."

Hadn't she done exactly the same? "Me, too."

"Only I made the promise five thousand times a day, a
least," Cam continued, like kissing her was some kind c
onus crime. "Do not kiss Meredith Brennan. Do not kis
Meredith—"

"I get it." She tried to pull back, but he held tight.

"But I can't help but want to kiss Meredith Brennan," h
whispered, his soft breath teasing her neck, her ear. "An

that's a problem because we've got history, we're working together, and I don't want to mess things up."

She took a broad step back. This time he let her go, but one hand came up and cradled her face, her cheek. "Sorry. You just looked so cute, all self-righteous and jealous, and I..." he shrugged "...couldn't help myself."

"First of all." She held up one newly manicured pointer finger. "I was neither self-righteous nor jealous."

He barked a quick laugh, then clapped a hand across his mouth. "Of course not."

"Secondly." She added another finger. "You're right. We've got a working relationship we shouldn't mess up, but the last time I looked we were both adults. Adults can actually balance things, Cam Calhoun, because they're grown-ups." She leaned in, planted a quick kiss on his very surprised face, then stepped back and lifted the cookie tray. "I'm not seventeen anymore. Neither are you. And because it's not exactly a crime to kiss each other, I suggest we do it now and again. Just to see."

She'd surprised him. No, wait, make that totally stupefied him if the look on his face was any indication. Well, good. For once she was going to take the upper hand. Grasp her destiny. Take charge.

Right after she showed up late at her mother's house and explained to the family why she was tardy, carefully leaving Cam out of the equation. But with Heather and Rory there, her mother would know something was up, because not much got past Dana Brennan, and she'd left Heather's place over a half-hour before.

She turned at the door. "You hungry?"

Head angled, Cam contemplated her. A tiny smile quirked the left side of his jaw. "Nah. You go. Have fun. We'll talk soon."

"Okay."

Talk, Mere. Keep it friendly and casual. Do not, I repeat, do not go off the deep end over your old boyfriend just because his kiss wiped all traces of coherent thought from your brain, and the woodsy scent of him turned your insides to mush. You've got time. Take time. No more rushing headlong into love or anything else. Got it?

Oh, she got it all right. And she knew better. As she climbed back into her run-of-the-mill sedan, she thought of Haley Jennings and the candy-apple-red sports car. Younger. Beautiful. Blonde. Ambitious. And she probably hadn't had a two-year-long affair with a senator's husband.

Guilt stabbed, making her reconsider her edict to Cam.

Images of Sophie and Rachel swam in her brain. Two precious girls, impressionable. They didn't need to walk in the shadows of her past, not now, not ever. Meredith wasn't foolish. She understood the workings of Washington better than most. If someone decided they wanted news of her relationship with Chas/Charles to come out, it would, and Sylvia Bellwater was up for reelection in November. What better way for the opposing party to thwart her efforts than a smear campaign. And if that happened, she would be in the thick of it, named or unnamed. And in D.C. circles, the unnamed always got identified in the end.

She pulled into her mother's drive, relieved to see Matt and Callie climbing out of their car just ahead. If half the party was late, she wouldn't feel quite so guilty. Or alone.

But knowing that what just happened with Cam shouldn't happen again, made her feel more alone than ever.

Chapter Eight

She was avoiding him.

For nearly a week he'd been in and out of Stillwaters at night with no glimpse of Meredith. Oh, she'd been there, all right, just not when he was around. The pedicure room moldings wore a blush of soft, sage-green against dusk-rose walls. The old paper in the turret room was gone and fresh cream-colored paint brightened the arced walls. The upstairs hall had been repainted as well, a blend of café au lait and mauve, and she'd left tiles for him to examine, to make a decision on the flooring.

With a terse note.

He sighed, examined the choices, then hit her phone number, and wasn't surprised when it went to voice mail on the fourth ring.

The kiss, no doubt.

Well, that was fine, because he'd been doing some reconsidering of his own, wondering what had gotten into him. What made him take that bold step forward? Was it her mouth, the memory of his lips on hers from days of old, wondering if it would be the same?

It wasn't the same, it was better. And that spelled trouble all around.

Maybe he was drawn by the pale sweep of her cheek, a profile that hinted sorrow and pain? The saucy hair, a nest of curls, clipped back but wild and untamable?

All of the above, he realized. But he shoved the knowledge aside, determined to move on.

His phone rang. He glanced down and felt a pang of regret that it wasn't Meredith's number in his display. "Hey, Mom. What's up?"

"Are you picking me up tomorrow?"

Tomorrow?

Cam cringed, fought a scowl at his memory lapse and nodded, unseen. "Yes. The girls and I will be by at nine-thirty."

"That won't work. Susan Langley called me."

"From The Edge?" Susan Langley and her husband Gary owned the lovely hillside restaurant overlooking the Jamison Valley.

"Yes, but she called because she's on the ecumenical council and they're organizing the food for the Easter egg hunt. I said I'd help."

Cam reached up to clean his ear, then shifted the tiny phone's receiver. "You what?"

"I'm helping serve food at the egg hunt tomorrow." She huffed the words as if his reaction surprised her. Cam couldn't remember the last time his mother voluntarily stepped outside of her comfort zone, an area that included the four solid walls of her small ranch house.

"So what time do you need to be there?" He hid the tone of amazement with a master's skill.

"Nine o'clock."

"Then we'll come at eight-forty-five."

"Fine. But you'll have to find something to do for an hour," she added, insistent. "The kids aren't supposed to get there until a quarter of ten."

"Got it."

"And don't spend money feeding them when there will be perfectly good food right there."

One, two, three...

Cam unclenched his jaw, but it took way more effort than it should have. "I'll take care of it, Mom. See you in the morning."

"Don't be late."

He hung up without saying goodbye, before he said something he'd regret. She was his mother.

But he'd stopped being a kid a long time ago, and her bossy, antagonistic nature pushed people away, leaving her more alone as she aged. He knew it was her own fault, but having her alone and lonely weighed on him.

And here she was, out of the blue, reaching out to the community. Would wonders never cease?

"Susan, good morning." Meredith entered the spacious kitchen behind the Gathering Hall and grabbed an apron. "Point me where you need me to go."

Susan Langley smiled a welcome, handed off a tray of empty coffee carafes and hooked a thumb left. "I'm putting the prettiest helpers on coffee service, Meredith, so if you'd be so kind as to find Alyssa, you can help her get set up. We're doing coffee in the back corner because food will be going in and out of the kitchen all morning."

"Perfectly planned as always." Meredith reached over, gave the older woman a quick hug and pushed through the Dutch door to check the morning's progress.

The newly renovated youth center bustled with activity. She spotted Alyssa Michaels on the far side and headed her way as her sister-in-law, Callie, met up with them from the other direction. "We're all on coffee duty? Sweet."

"And juice." Alyssa indicated trays of juice boxes and more adult versions of orange juice in tall, acrylic pitchers. "Do you think we need all three of us here?"

Meredith splayed her hands up, palms out. "Oh, do not go there. When your mother gives a direction, I follow. She sent me here, so here's where I'm staying."

Callie didn't disagree. "Ditto. Strong matriarchs are to be respected at all costs and double that at community functions."

"You guys know my mother well." Alyssa swept the room a glance, then shrugged. "And we got an outpouring of help for this little shindig, so we'll just man our coffeepots and have fun dishing about what's new." She settled a deliberately lazy look at Callie's midsection and hiked a brow. "You first, Callie."

Callie laughed. "There is no such thing as a secret in a small town. Who needs a JumboTron when we've got neighbors?"

Alyssa filled a tray with paper cups of orange juice. "Amen to that. When?"

"If all goes well, and we're praying it does…"

Alyssa sent a nod of first trimester understanding.

"Thanksgiving."

"Such a wonderful time for a perfect blessing, Cal."

Callie sent a skeptical look to her right. "The smell of that bacon and sausage might prove too much for me. If I duck out the back door—" she indicated the emergency exit behind their coffee service "—it will only be for a little fresh air. Cooking meat doesn't happen in our house right now. Matt either grills outside or we eat pasta. With plain red sauce or cheese. And yes, I am that boring."

"Whatever it takes." Meredith slipped an arm around Callie and half hugged her. "I can't wait to see this baby. Hold him. Or her."

"And with two of them on the way…"

"We'll be busy," Meredith added. She started filling the coffee carafes from the stadium-type urns against the wall.

"Two?" Alyssa turned, surprised. "Hannah, too? Oh, that's

delightful. And just last year I was lamenting that we didn't have enough young mothers around here to shake a stick at, and look what's happened."

"I am not drinking the water in this town." Meredith made the point-blank statement from her spot at the wall. "It's obviously potent and dangerous."

Alyssa moved closer and kept her voice low. "Not as potent and dangerous as working arm in arm with an old boyfriend, I'd wager. So tell us, Meredith…" She stretched the words out long and slow. "How are things going at the Senator's Mansion? With Cam?"

"I barely see him." Meredith kept her tone quick and light, but from the exchanged looks, she knew she wasn't fooling these women. "I make sure I work around his hours so it doesn't get awkward."

"Which means it's already gotten awkward," Callie said. She tapped one finger along the side of her face. "And awkward almost always means a kiss. Or two."

"At least two," agreed Alyssa.

"Stop."

"Two," Callie decided.

"I concur," added Alyssa. She leaned closer, as if she wasn't close enough already, hovering over Meredith's shoulder. "So…how was it?"

"What?"

"The kiss." Callie stepped closer, too. "And I'll bet it was last week before dinner at your mother's place because a, you were late and, b, you were flushed and, c…"

Meredith handed off a full carafe of regular coffee and shifted her attention to the growing line of people. "Off-limits discussion and we've got people needing caffeine."

Alyssa bent for the second carafe and whispered, "This conversation is not over."

"Oh, it is," Meredith assured her. "My vow of silence confirms that."

Busy now, Alyssa grabbed the decaf pot and moved down the table to fill coffee cups while Meredith continued to fill carafes.

She'd forgotten how good it felt to laugh and tease with her colleagues and friends. She'd had few friends at the spa. It was hard to form strong bonds when you were the boss because complaints of favoritism ran rampant. Remembering Heather's stand on that, she realized again how she might have done things differently.

At Stillwaters, she would. With Heather's help and straightforward approach, a work crew would start out on the right foot. Meredith recognized the wisdom therein. Taking over the operation in Maryland meant she absorbed old problems as the woman in charge. Here? A fresh start. On multiple fronts.

"Meredith, hi!"

"Hi, Meredith."

Two excited voices hailed her from the middle of the room, accompanied by a totally cute dad, looking way too good in work boots and blue jeans. Bookended by the two precious and precocious girls, Cam's grin made the bright, new room pale in comparison.

"Coffee. You're a lifesaver, Mere."

She raised the just-filled carafe and grasped a cup the same moment his hand went for it, then tried to pretend his hand on hers meant nothing, that a ping of sweet sensation didn't wrangle its way up her arm and settle somewhere in the vicinity of her heart.

He felt it, too. The grin widened. The sky-blue eyes crinkled and laugh lines that didn't see enough use made him seem less scholarly, quite approachable. The feel of his hand magnified the effect and she was pretty sure she'd inadvertently pour coffee on his hand instead of into the cup if he didn't let go.

"Allow me." Keeping his gaze on hers, he took the carafe

while the girls helped themselves to juice boxes, and oh-so-slowly poured his coffee, her hand still trapped beneath his.

Alyssa smiled.

Callie cleared her throat with meaning.

And Meredith realized that going eight days without seeing Cam, talking to Cam, working with Cam had done nothing but raise the stakes. And funny, with him right there, her hand between his and the foam cup, she didn't feel scared. Or concerned. Looking at Cam, gazing into his eyes, a tiny direct connection of protection and care bore into her heart, her soul.

"I suppose if I want to drink this coffee..." He shifted forward a little, halving their already narrow separation. "I need to let go so you can let go."

"And if I don't want to?"

He straightened, released her hand, then accepted the full cup while he met her gaze straight on. "Then you have a pretty funny way of showing it, Mere. Day nine of being ignored, avoided and shut out."

His direct approach deserved nothing less in return. "Running scared."

He shrugged and the next comment cut deep because of its veracity. "What else is new?"

She hated that he was right. And that he called her on it. Especially when her choices hinged on protecting his daughters. And him. But he'd never know that and she wasn't about to make excuses. "True enough. But while I'm here to stay this time, I'm not in the market for anything other than work."

He tipped his cup in salute and angled his head while the girls busied themselves with doughnut holes from the Tops Market in Wellsville. "Not what you said last week."

"I was being impetuous."

He nodded and sent her a serious look, one that meant business. "I wasn't. But I appreciate the heads-up. Strictly business from this point forward. Got it."

He turned to head toward the girls as the big room filled

with anxious, excited egg-hunters and their parents, then swung back. "When we're not kissing, that is."

Alyssa's grin said she heard and approved.

Callie's laugh agreed.

He didn't wait for Meredith's rebuttal, and she remembered that Cam's timing had always been spot-on. Which meant his calm, cool facade was often hiding the man within, a man who managed to touch her heart and soul in the past few weeks.

He disappeared outside with the girls. Luckily the crowd looking for coffee and juices kept her busy enough to not notice his absence, not long for his deep voice, his gaze of amused affection. The quiet persona that said so much.

He'd called her a gypsy last week. And it probably seemed that way to him, that she'd traipsed around, seeking fulfillment in her quest for success. That journey had tripped her up, but it also allowed her to develop some wonderful skills along the way. Skills she'd use here in her hometown.

By the time the egg hunt had concluded and clean-up was nearly done, she realized that being part of a community service event like this felt good. Real good. Right until Evelyn Calhoun cornered her outside the ladies' room. "Meredith."

She knew that voice. A little more querulous, perhaps, but still dogmatic. Tough. Acerbic.

Which only meant she'd smile brighter. Longer.

She turned and met the older woman's tight gaze. "Mrs. Calhoun. How nice to see you."

Evelyn took a bold step forward. "You're working with my son."

Um, your thirty-four-year-old son, plenty old enough to be taking care of himself. Meredith flashed perfect cheerleader teeth. "And loving it. Cam's amazingly talented, and those girls, well—" She raised her shoulders. "How could anyone not fall in love with those girls?"

Evelyn's eyes narrowed. Her lips thinned. Dark, shaggy

brows drew close over the bridge of her nose. "Them girls don't need to be all gussied up, their heads filled with all kinds of nonsense. They're smart and have the common sense of their mother and I don't want you messing with that."

Meredith saw two options. Spar with the old woman and risk starting a war.

Or...

Keep her peace, beg off and go home.

War won.

"Cam's a grown man." Meredith kept her voice firm but soft. "I'm a grown woman. And no one has the right to tell us what to do or how to do it, so let's make sure that's clear right up front, okay?"

Evelyn's scowl deepened, but surprise lightened her eyes. She obviously hadn't anticipated any kind of rebuttal.

Welcome to the new millennium, Mrs. C.

"Secondly, my work isn't nonsense. Taking care of one's body, one's appearance and one's skin makes perfect sense in a world filled with prevalent toxins. Wellness involves the whole body, one unit of many parts. If you ignore any of those parts, others pay the price. And skin makes up a larger percentage of the human body than any other component." She drew a breath, figuring she might never get the chance to go one-on-one with Evelyn Calhoun again because she was pretty sure Cam's mother would never be darkening the door of Stillwaters or inviting her for tea. "And lastly, respect is a two-way street. Those who desire respect need to show it in return."

She spun on her heel and strode away, not waiting for Evelyn's response. As a teen she'd have cowered before the verbal onslaught, but now?

Mutual respect was expected.

"Whoa."

Alyssa grabbed her arm inside the Gathering Hall door. "Did you just face down the dragon lady?"

A thread of regret wound alongside the spur of adrenaline. "I did. But I probably shouldn't have."

"Yes, you should." Alyssa tugged her forward, away from others. "No one's got the right to treat you like that, Meredith. Being old doesn't give Evelyn the right to be rude and antagonistic. And you weren't disrespectful, you were simply…" she searched for a word, then shrugged and grinned "…downright amazing."

Meredith laughed, then sighed, chagrined. Treating Cam's mother like a naughty teen might not score points, but she'd promised herself to take charge of her life when she made the decision to leave Maryland.

And that included Evelyn Calhoun. And Jacqui Crosby. And Claire Dennehy, and anyone else who sharpened their tongue at her expense. It would be sinful to hold a grudge over wrongs long past, but standing up for herself? Taking charge?

God had no problem with that.

"Girls, thank you!" Susan waved a hand their way from the kitchen. "I couldn't have gotten this put together and served without your help. So be prepared to be tagged in any Facebook event I might send out, okay?"

Alyssa and Meredith laughed. "Will do, Mom." Alyssa turned back toward Meredith. "And don't be worrying about Mrs. Calhoun. She acted. You reacted. Pure science, beginning to end."

"Thanks, Alyssa." She gave the other woman a quick hug of gratitude, knowing Alyssa had faced her own dragons back in the day. "Gotta run. I'm working with Heather this afternoon and then stripping wallpaper tonight."

"Have fun."

"I will."

And she would, Meredith realized. Yes, she felt bad about sparring with Evelyn on one level, but glad she stood up for herself. Stillwaters Spa would be beneficial to this village, this town, this county, and she had every intention of making sure people knew that. And if quieting sharp tongues was part of her job, well…so be it. What had Heather advised her? That infighting wouldn't be allowed. And that edict included the terse, curt tongues of some older locals.

Chapter Nine

Meredith eyed the clock on Sunday morning, squinched her eyes shut, then forced them open again.

Seven-twenty-five. Church was at nine. And she'd promised her mother they'd go together, which meant the eleven o'clock service wasn't an option.

She stretched, then scowled, the pain in her shoulders a reminder of scrubbing off acres of ugly, ornate wallpaper the night before. She and Heather had worked until midnight, but they'd gotten the stuff off, shoveled it into waiting garbage bins and cleaned the floor. This afternoon she could sand and paint the walls.

Her walls.

That realization lessened the aches and pains of manual labor. Her phone signaled a text as she dressed. She eyed the number, and tried to ignore the skipped beat of her heart.

Cam.

Are you working this afternoon?

Meredith loved that he didn't use text-speak, the acronym-heavy way of replacing words with letters. Spelling things out seemed more Cam-like.

Yes.

His answer came back swiftly, as if he was waiting for her.

Would you prefer I didn't work today?

Not work? What?

Then she realized the foolishness of her actions. Her prickly attitude would end up costing them valuable work time if she wasn't careful. She quickly typed back:

It's a big house. Plenty of room.

Did he smile? Grin? Scowl?

Impossible to know via text messaging. Ridiculous, even. No way could she get a read on him, his tone, the subtle silences that weighed his conversations.

Worse, she couldn't hear his voice. Irritated, she dialed his number and waited four rings before he picked up.

Four.

And she was relatively certain he was standing there, phone in hand, making her wait on purpose. Which only tweaked her more. When he finally answered the phone, she was in rare form, but his first words took the wind out of her sails. "I was wondering how long it would take."

"For?"

His voice bore traces of the smile she knew so well. "You to call. To want to hear my voice. Like I want to hear yours."

"Cameron Calhoun—"

"The girls are going to church with a friend from up the road. I'm free from eleven on, so I figured I'd continue on the hairdressing side. But then I have to wait for the electric upgrades before I can go much further and that could take up to two weeks. Following that, the fire chief has to assess the installations to make sure everything is done according to code."

"Two weeks? Really? So we're at a standstill until that's done?"

"Until that's done and inspected," he told her. "But in the meantime I'm going to make the built-in cabinetry on the side porch and a lot of that can be done while we're waiting for the electrical and plumbing upgrades. Who's doing the bathrooms?"

"Allegany Plumbing and Heating."

"Excellent. I've worked with Bob on a lot of projects. So I'm going to map out a time frame for you. If you're more comfortable being there when I'm not there, this will help."

Right now she felt like an adolescent jerk for making a big deal out of a kiss she'd not only enjoyed, but followed up on. "It's fine, Cam. I overreacted."

Silence. Dead silence.

"It won't happen again," she promised.

"The overreacting or the kiss?"

"Either."

His subsequent laugh said he doubted both, but instead of setting her off, it made her smile. Cam knew her, had known her, for a long time. He understood the occasional manic moments and had calmly waited in the wings for them to pass. She'd been a teenage drama queen in many regards. Sure, some of the blame lay with her father, her family situation. But the bulk of it?

On her shoulders. What had Alyssa said? Action/reaction.

Grown-ups needed to separate emotional reactions from business transactions, and if she intended to build a successful enterprise here, she needed to man up. If that meant working around Cam repeatedly, then that's what she'd do. "So I'll see you later, then."

"Will do." He disconnected and she stood there, caught in place, in time, studying the phone as if it held all the answers.

"Mere? You ready?" Dana's voice interrupted her moment of reverie.

"Um, yes. Almost. Kind of."

Dana laughed. "I'm starting the car. It's raining again."

"April showers…"

"Ruin good hair," her mother filled in. "Luckily I have a live-in hairdresser."

Meredith hurried down the stairs of the classic old colonial, grabbed a light cape, and drew it around her shoulders.

"You look like a Celtic princess when you wear that." Dana's easy smile said she approved.

"Not too Druid-like for Jamison?"

"No, ma'am. It's gorgeous. Just made for long legs and long hair. If I tried to wear a getup like that?" Dana waved a hand to Meredith's ankle-length, emerald-green cape. "I'd look like an elf."

"An adorable elf, though."

"Well, thank you. So—" Dana curved toward Route 19 and headed north. "I think we'll aim for the White Church at the Bend today."

"I love Simon's preaching. And Katie's hand at the fiddle."

"Amazing," her mother agreed. "And I promised Simon financial support for their remodeling project."

"His 'Replace The Buckets' campaign?" The small church with a growing congregation was in desperate need of repair. Matt and his crew had patched the roof last fall, but the whole thing needed a removal-to-bare-bones overhaul to fix the roof and the damage done by leaking water.

Dana laughed. "New roof, new ceiling and new lighting and paint to brighten up the old place. I figure if this new young preacher is lighting hearts on fire for God, the least I can do is help pay to light up the church they attend."

"You're amazing, Mom."

Dana shrugged that off.

"No, I mean it." Meredith swiveled more fully in her seat. "You care. And then you act. You're not all talk and no action, and your example is wonderful to me and everyone else."

"Well."

Her mother hated talking about herself. Always had. And while a lot of folks had gossiped at Dana's expense in the past, she never held a grudge. And that was a lesson Meredith needed to embrace.

"I admire you, Mom."

Dana's profile shaded. She pulled into the parking lot behind the humble white church, stopped the car and faced Meredith. "It's payback, pure and simple. Your father hurt a lot of people with his actions. And for a long time, business suffered, the family suffered and the towns suffered. Now?" She shrugged, her voice matter-of-fact, her face showing strength through acquired peace. "Business is good. Most of your father's greed has been paid back to various factions, and I want to wipe the slate clean. Walk through town with my head up, eyes forward and not worry about gossip."

So her mother wasn't the brick wall Meredith had thought her to be. "But you never let on that it bothered you. Ever."

Dana settled a gentle look on her daughter. "Because that would empower them. Give them more ammunition. Feed the flames."

Meredith reached across the car and gave her mother a quick hug. "I love you. I wish I was more like you, but I'm trying. Really hard."

Dana hugged her back, and might have sniffled back a tear. Maybe two. "Look at us, all emotional and silly. But hear this, my beautiful girl—I love having you home. I missed you every day that you were gone, but a parent's job isn't to cocoon their child. It's to help them establish roots and develop those wings we keep hearing about. And you've done both, Mere. I'm proud of you."

Her mother's words felt good. Sounded good. But that tiny spear knifed Meredith's heart a little more. Her mother wouldn't be so proud if she knew what had pushed Meredith home. That knowledge would only paint the portrait of Neal Brennan's daughter darker and deeper. Like father, like daughter.

You were duped, her conscience chided. *Fooled in love.*

Yes and no, Meredith decided. Fooled, yes. But adults were expected to take responsibility for their own actions.

She grasped her mother's arm, planted a kiss on the smaller woman's cheek and headed into the worn but wonderful church, ready to hear Simon MacDaniel's take on Christ's passion and suffering the week before Easter.

"Mere, you here?" Cam hesitated inside the door of the old mansion as prickling awareness snaked his spine later that day. No car. No music. No footsteps overhead. And yet something, a soft, repetitive whooshing sound, seemed to be coming from…somewhere. Void of furniture, noises echoed in the old place, bouncing off high-ceilinged walls like a mountain cove. "Mere?"

"Cam, is that you?"

It was him, but the moment she appeared at the top of the stairs, paint roller in hand, old paint sweats disguising her curves, his heart tipped in a way he'd thought long forgotten.

Obviously not.

"You're painting." *Duh, Cameron. State the obvious, why don't you?*

A smile brightened her face. She slid her gaze slowly and dramatically toward the paint roller without moving her head. "Yes. I am."

He laughed at himself and her. "No car."

She hiked one shoulder. "Mom dropped me off. Her car's acting weird. I told her I was going to be here for the day and so she's meeting with Simon and Matt about the church fix-up."

"Simon?"

Mere jerked her head toward the back of the hall. "Come up here a minute to talk. My paint's getting tacky."

Cam knew he shouldn't. He'd been going back and forth about this as he sketched out custom cupboard measurements, while the girls were gone, the house quiet.

But he took the stairs two at a time because he couldn't resist the invitation. He stopped at the entrance to a grandiose bedroom and turned in a slow circle. "You've been busy."

She nodded, satisfied as she refreshed the roller. "Heather and I stripped the walls yesterday. Made for a late night, but it's done. And then I sanded it this morning after church, cut in along the amazing number of edges you see here, and now I'm ready to roll."

"And the paint color is perfect," he noted.

"You think?"

He nodded, serious. "Light enough to brighten this big space and it sets off the mahogany panels beautifully. That's important in old places with dark wood."

"Thank you, Cam."

She turned and continued applying the pale rose paint to the wall and he couldn't help but appreciate the care she took to feather each stroke into the adjacent space. A good painter never rushed their work or used mucked-up tools, and Meredith obviously embraced that philosophy.

"Who's Simon?"

She finished a long, slow stroke along the edge of the adjacent door frame and he tried to ignore the beauty of the move. Or maybe it was the woman doing it. Either way, he was having a hard time concentrating, which was exactly why he should have stayed home. Or on the first floor. Or preferably on the porch with the door locked.

He sighed inside, then schooled his looks into a semblance of nonchalance when she turned.

"You don't know Simon MacDaniel?"

He shook his head.

"He's the pastor at the White Church at the Bend."

"Oh."

"I know you guys probably still go to Good Shepherd across the Park Round, but his name's outside on the welcome sign. I just figured you'd have noticed."

"No."

He might have noticed if he darkened the doors of a church more often, but he'd been more than a little lax in that area for a long time now. He wasn't much in the line of praying, in any case, so—

"He's just a sweetheart." Mere continued to fill him in on details as she reloaded the roller for the next square of plaster. "So funny. Mom and I have been making the rounds of churches since I've been back. It's kind of fun and ecumenical to jump from place to place each week. Hear different ideas on similar topics."

"The girls were at Good Shepherd with the Monroes this morning."

"Ah." She paused her work this time, then turned, her expression deeper. More thoughtful. "And you?"

He waved the clutch of papers in his hand. "Working out the final cabinet design for the hairdressing side. Then we'll get to work on the spa rooms. The pedicure unit. And the nail stations."

"You used to go to church all the time." Meredith's tone held no hint of reproval, so why did he feel guilty?

Because he'd been feeling guilty for five years, minimum. Why should now be any different? And he took the girls himself on occasion, but each time he stepped foot into a house of God, and it didn't matter which one he went to, he remembered Kristy's simple faith in God and him.

They'd both failed her miserably. And he hated being reminded of that. "Life's crazy busy. The girls. Two jobs. Keeping things up at home."

She flashed him a look of understanding that drove the guilt deeper. "It's got to be hard, Cam. But you're doing a great job, if the girls are any indication." She turned back to the wall while she continued her work.

"I think Mom and Grandma are financing the refurbishing of Simon's church," she continued. "With others, of course. Their congregation is small, and if people donate time to help with the work, Mom's ready to write a sizable check to offset the supplies."

"Your mother's great."

"She is." Meredith nodded and smiled. "I didn't realize how great when I was a kid, but now, well..." She shrugged one shoulder. "Amazing how perspectives change as a grown-up."

"Yes. Well." Cam swiped damp palms against his pants. Watching her, he realized not everything changed once you grew up. Seeing her work, hearing her voice, watching her move, he longed to be with her just as much as he had at eighteen. More, maybe. Memories of school dances, weekend *feises,* football games, cheerleading moves...

Stop. Now.

He whacked himself upside the head internally, turned and headed for the stairs. "Gotta get busy. The Monroes are keeping the girls until six, so I've got solid work time. Don't want to mess with that."

"No." She smiled his way, and he wondered if she had any idea what that meant to him. Her support, her acceptance. For some reason, it mattered. A lot. But despite Meredith's promises to stay, she'd only been back a few months and Cam couldn't deny the thought that if the going got tough, Meredith might head for the hills. Sure, she was older. More mature. And still gorgeous.

That indiscriminate thought made him both grin and grimace as he descended the stairs.

But he had two little girls who didn't need or want more heartache. He'd made a promise to himself that their lives would be rock-solid. Full. Vibrant. Letting them get too attached to Meredith could be a big mistake.

But that smile…

Meredith appeared at the porch door several hours later. She had coffee in one hand and a box in the other. "Danish and fry pies from Seb Walker's place. Mom and I stopped this morning after church."

Cam didn't hesitate. "And you waited until now to tell me they were here?"

She proffered the box and took a seat on a board slung across two five-gallon buckets. "Didn't want to interrupt your work, but since Sunday afternoon dinner time has come and gone, these kept calling my name."

"Delicious." He reached for a pastry as she did. Their knuckles bumped. Then paused. Then bumped again, right before his fingers twined around hers. "Mere."

She kept her gaze trained on their interlocked hands. "They fit."

"Always did."

A tiny smile curved her left cheek up. "But then we grew up, Cam."

He squeezed her fingers lightly. "And we stayed grown-up."

"But grown-up means we have a past," she told him. Her words didn't say as much as her lifted gaze, the sorrow he read behind those dark blue irises.

"And a present and a future," he shot back. He grabbed a cheese-filled Italian pastry, tested the propped board for weight, then sat down next to her. "Everyone's got a past, right?"

She nodded.

"And we're working together in the present, correct?"

"Yes."

"So I suggest we take this day by day, interspersed with the more-than-occasional kiss and see where it leads." He leaned over and feathered a gentle touch to her mouth with his lips, the combination of sweet cheese and fresh coffee delightful. "Because I like kissing you, Mere. A lot."

She sat back and shot him a bemused look. "Me, too. Which can only mean one thing, Cam."

"We kiss more and see where this leads us?" He grinned, and resolved to ignore the warning flashes exploding in his head. Yes, falling for Meredith would be risky. But since he'd survived once, maybe he could do it again.

But the girls, his conscience implored. *What about the girls? Didn't you just go through, step by step, the reasons to avoid Meredith Brennan?*

He had, he decided as his lips resettled on hers. But somehow, when he was in her presence, all rational thought managed to fly out the window. And the fact that she returned the kiss…it meant she wasn't nearly as staunch and stalwart as she pretended to be, and he liked that. A lot.

The sound of a car engine interrupted them.

"The girls are here."

Meredith sat back, a frown marring the classic lines of her face. "Yes."

"Mere."

"Cam." She stood, straightened, and sent him a look that wounded. Or was the look itself wounded? He wasn't sure, but knew one thing. Something pained her. Bothered her. Old wrongs? Secrets? There'd been so many back in the day, with Neal Brennan's tomcat-prowling making tongues wag, including his mother's. And she'd been sensitive to it. Overly, maybe, but then how could he say? No one used his family as gossip fodder. And he was a man. Maybe that stuff sat different with women.

"Hey, Dad! Meredith! We had so much fun with Ellie and Isaac!"

W

e'd like to send you two free books to introduce you to the Love Inspired® series. Your two books have a combined cover price of $11.50 or more in the U.S. and $13.50 or more in Canada, but they are yours to keep absolutely FREE! We'll even send you two wonderful surprise gifts. You can't lose!

The Reader Service — Here's How it Works:

Cam caught Rachel in a hug. Sophie followed more slowly, a clear sign that something was wrong. "What's up, Soph?"

She shook her head. "I don't feel so good."

"You don't?"

"No?"

He and Mere bent in unison. Mere took the little girl's hand and Cam laid his cool palm against a very hot brow. "You've got a fever, honey."

"Do I?"

She peered at him glassy-eyed and he felt that old familiar clutch to his gut, the one that reminded him of finding Kristy cold and lifeless on the living room couch. That stark image was forever burned in his brain, epitaphed by his self-concern.

He hated the man he was back then.

He wasn't all that pleased with himself now.

"Come on, honey. Let's get you home. Why didn't you call me? I'd have come right over and picked you up."

"I didn't know," she told him honestly. "I thought I was just tired. And I was worried about Sally the kitten, and that made me sad."

The kitten. Cam slammed himself internally. He'd promised her he'd take time to hunt for the tiny cat, and then he'd gotten tied up in work and forgot. What kind of a lame father was he?

"That happens." Mere leaned down and feathered a kiss to her brow, then grasped Rachel's hand. "I'll walk out with Rachel and you bring Sophie. And I'll clean up in there." She wagged her head toward the side porch.

"I'll put the tools away. They're heavy."

"You'll take your precious daughter home and tuck her in with some ibuprofen, hot lemonade and a story." She gave the order lightly, but Cam read the no-nonsense look in her eye. "Matt's coming by in an hour and I'll have him put the heavy stuff back in the kitchen area. Okay?"

"Yes. Thank you. I—"

She touched the back of his hand, a whisper of a touch, but enough. Just enough to make him feel less alone. Less guilty. Less laden. "I'll be praying that this virus is a quick twenty-four-hour thing and she's good as new by morning."

She'd be praying. For him. For Sophie.

People had offered him prayers for years, from every local denomination. He'd smiled politely, thanked them and moved on, knowing what God knew: he'd neglected to take care of his wife.

But when Mere uttered those words, promising her petition…something warm and flowing stirred inside him again, like a rusted iron faucet being urged back to life, the tiny trickle of water a good sign.

"Goodbye, honey." She leaned in and gave Rachel a quick kiss and then squeezed Sophie's hand. "Bless you, darling. Get well quick, okay?"

"I will, Mere."

Sophie's tiny reply pushed Cam home quickly. The girls had been sick before. His head knew that childhood illness came on in a flash and could leave just as quickly.

But his heart went a little stale each time. He couldn't afford to be cool and casual about things like fevers and congestion, no matter what his head said, because his heart couldn't possibly bear another mistake.

Chapter Ten

Meredith called Cam first thing the next morning, realized she'd woken him and almost felt bad. But not quite. "How's she doing?"

"Who is this?"

"Meredith. Stop messing with me, Cam. How's Sophie?"

She heard him yawn and imagined him stretching, then immediately tried to wipe that image from her mind.

Too late.

"Sleeping right now. Like I was."

"Sorry."

He laughed. "Don't be. I've got to get Rachel on the bus in forty-five minutes so I had to get up anyway."

"And Rachel's fine so far?"

"No sign of it yet, but that means she'll probably get sick later in the week."

"And you're staying home with Sophie?"

"Of course."

His tone went too sharp for her liking, sick kid or not. "Don't bark at me. I was just asking. Heather and I are working at the spa today and they're starting the bathroom tear-out tomorrow, so if you need me to watch her tomorrow, that would be fine. Mom would be there, too, and between the two of us, we could probably manage one nine-year-old. Then you can go to work."

"I've got it, thanks."

"Okay." His tight tone niggled more than the words. "Give her my best and if you need anything—"

"We're good, but I appreciate the offer."

Sure he did. Like Florida appreciates a Category Four hurricane warning. She hung up, wondering what that was all about. One minute he was kissing her, the next he was shouldering her aside, blocking her offers of help.

Whatever.

She'd headed for Stillwaters without her second cup of coffee, so when she swung into the parking lot at Heather's place she was more than a little out of sorts. She'd decided to stay away from Cam and it had worked for over a week. Why had she let down her reserve yesterday? Was she a glutton for punishment? Obviously so.

His quick dismissal had put her firmly in her place, which was right where she should be, avoiding him and entanglements with those two little girls at all costs.

Jerk.

"You need coffee, and you need it bad." Heather made the observation as she tied a bandanna around her head to protect her hair from paint mist. They were rolling the bedroom ceilings at the Senator's Mansion today, a shoulder-numbing job, and even with the protective roller covers, some paint mist would fill the air.

"Thank you for noticing." Meredith grabbed the pot, filled her cup, laced it with sugar and chocolate/coconut creamer, stirred, sniffed and tasted. "Perfect. You may have just saved someone's life. Good job, Heather."

"Cam's, I presume."

Meredith shot her a dark look.

Heather laughed. "Hard to maintain your distance, huh? Obey your own edicts?"

"I did fine until yesterday. Then I messed up. But I've been reminded that I need to stay on my side of the great divide. The man's got some kind of ax to grind and I don't intend to be the target."

"Cam?" Heather frowned. "Cam Calhoun is about the most patient, easygoing guy I've ever met. What did you do to him?"

Mere arched forward in pretend anger. "That's just it. Not a thing. Not one blessed thing. There we were, eating pastries and kissing, and the next thing I know Sophie's sick and he turns into the dragon-master."

"Oh."

"Oh, what? Like, that's normal? Like, that's something? Because it's not," Meredith expounded. "Kids get sick all the time, it's not exactly life-threatening, right?"

Heather grimaced. "His wife died of pneumonia. Right there at home. She went to sleep one night and never woke up. They thought it was a bad cold. A rhinovirus that was going around, but it took a bad turn in Kristy. So he's a little sensitive, I bet. Possibly bordering on neurotic."

That image caught Meredith up short. "Pneumonia? In this day and age?"

Heather nodded, sympathetic. "Weird things happen. I guess she'd had a problem when she was little, and her lungs just couldn't fight it off. And like I said, they thought it was just a cold. Rachel was a toddler and Sophie was in preschool and Cam was teaching and doing his restoration work on the side. Crazy busy, trying to make ends meet. Like most young families."

"So when the kids get sick…"

"It most likely drums up a whole lot of bad memories."

Of course it would. She envisioned Cam finding his wife deceased, the pain and the horror of that, his inability to help or spin back the hands of time. Then the daily reality of raising two little girls alone.

"I'll cut him some slack. I had no idea."

Heather shrugged. "He doesn't talk about it. Ever. But he does a great job with those girls. And his work is beyond comparison."

Meredith thought of the long stretch of cabinetry he'd installed yesterday. The steady hum of his saw. The precision-pumping of his drill as he applied holding screws. The knowledge that he was there, working, doing his best to make her dream come true.

He did do his best. She grabbed a to-go top for her coffee and headed for the door. "I'll take my angst out on the ceilings. And bring some ibuprofen. By tonight, we're going to need it."

"Not as much as you might think."

"No?" Meredith turned back.

Heather's expression said, "I know something you don't know." "I've got a plan. A wise woman always goes into a new venture with a plan."

"Is it legal? Please say yes."

Heather laughed out loud and climbed into Meredith's car. "Yes. But nothing this wonderful should be legal, because it's positively habit-forming. In a good way," she added, noting Meredith's mock scowl.

"Tell me you've got ibuprofen in your purse, just in case."

"I do."

"Then bring it on, Heather." Meredith popped the car into Drive and headed for the spa. "Whatever you've got, because by the end of the day, after four nine-foot ceilings, we're going to be in some righteous pain."

"I hear ya."

Meredith felt wonderful and it was all Heather's fault. And when she could remove herself from the cloud of bliss surrounding her now, she'd say so. But she managed to mumble

two little words that paused the hands massaging the sore-
ness out of her tired shoulders and upper back. "You're hired."

"I thought that might be the case." CeeCee Cummings
kept her voice low, the way a good massage therapist should.
"You don't want to see my credentials? My letters of recom-
mendation? My police record?"

At the moment, Meredith didn't care if CeeCee was Attila
the Hun and had transported herself through a time portal
buried on Dunnymeade Hill. She had magic hands and the
fire that had consumed Meredith's upper body couldn't even
be classified as a low flame now.

Reason enough right there to hire this woman. "Are you
a convict?"

CeeCee didn't hesitate. "No."

"Are you licensed?"

"Yes."

"Are you overpriced?"

"Most assuredly."

"But worth every penny," Heather stressed as she bagged
up the used rollers and headed for the door. "I'm putting the
garbage out. Pickup is tomorrow."

"I don't care. I'm sleepy." Thirty minutes ago she'd been in
pain and totally jacked on caffeine. Now? Ready for a good
night's sleep right here on the floor.

CeeCee finished her left shoulder and sat back. Meredith
propped one eye open, saw the honey-skinned woman's grin
of assessment, then eased herself to a sitting position. "There
are applications on the table inside the door."

"Done. Heather brought one to me yesterday."

"Awesome. Availability?"

A shadow darkened the pretty woman's eyes. "Whenever
you need me. I'm on my own. No clock to answer to except
a couple of adjustable lab shifts."

The time frame pleased Meredith, but she felt a stab of
empathy for whatever caused the shadow. "Wonderful. I'm

not sure what our need will be at this point. Where are you working now?"

"From home for the massage therapy. I do two shifts in the lab at the professional building adjacent to Jones Memorial Hospital. That keeps my benefits in place."

"What do you—"

CeeCee answered without waiting for the full question. "I draw blood. It keeps me in the medical game, requires little thought and no one dies."

Meredith's heart opened further. She'd respect CeeCee's privacy, but she understood tough, deep-seated emotion. "I hear you. So—" she rolled her shoulders and smiled at how much better they felt "—first, you're amazing. Second, yes, you really are hired unless you do have a record."

"I do not."

"Excellent." Meredith stood. "Third, if you have any preferences for your massage rooms, let me know."

"As in?"

"Equipment, lighting, setting."

"Soft light, relaxing music, ocean-waves soundtrack, warm tones."

Meredith laughed and clapped her on the back. "Done. And there will be a tea and juice service set up in the spa area. And the overseer will have video feed of the spa side at all times. She'll change the sheets, clean everything, service the beverages, maintain the lounge area and sweet-talk the customers that need it."

"It sounds wonderful. Thank you, Meredith." CeeCee offered her hand. "I'm grateful."

Meredith raised a hand to the back of her neck and smiled. "Me, too. I'll be in touch. We've got a couple of months yet, so…"

"I'll let my client base know." CeeCee met Meredith's look head-on. "Once I'm here, I won't freelance any longer."

Talk about a leap of faith. "CeeCee, I appreciate that, but I'm sure you've got bills to pay."

"Don't we all?" CeeCee hiked her purse higher on her shoulder. "But when someone gives you a hand up, I consider it bad manners to bite that hand."

"I love how you think."

The therapist settled a soft smile on Mere, and Mere realized she was younger than she first appeared. With old eyes. Knowing eyes. Eyes that saw too much. She reached out and gave the other woman an impulsive hug, and Meredith Brennan was not inclined to random hugging. "I'm looking forward to working with you."

"Thank you."

Meredith's phone rang as CeeCee moved toward the side door. When she saw Cam's number, she was tempted to let it go to voice mail, decided she was chicken-livered, and answered. "Hello, Cam. How's Sophie doing?"

"Better, but not ready for prime time. She needs another day home and Laura Henning just called from the high school. The building inspector is coming by tomorrow to give the approval on the project house."

"And you should be there."

"Exactly. Does your offer to watch Sophie still stand?"

When all else fails, err on the side of grace and kindness. Knowing more about Cam's history made that easier. "Of course. What time shall I come get her? Or would it be more comfortable if we watch her there?"

"She'd probably love coming to your mother's."

His quick reply said more than his words. "And you don't have time to clean your place tonight, right?"

"Smart girl. Not like that's a surprise. Can I drop her off at seven? Rachel can catch the bus at the neighbors' like they usually do because my day starts an hour earlier than theirs."

"Bring Rachel, too. I can feed them, then Mom can take Rachel to school. And it gives me a little time to spoil them."

"No pink."

She laughed out loud. "The very thought of a world without pink makes me shudder, Cameron, and you know that. I'm willfully ignoring your edict. Pink is my signature color."

Cam's voice went a little softer. A touch deeper. "You look great in anything, Mere."

She would not fall into the trap again. He had issues. She had issues. And never the twain shall meet.

"Thanks." She kept her tone light and brisk. "I'll see you in the morning, okay?"

He took two seconds too long, then went back to easy mode. "Perfect. See you then."

He hung up the phone, grimaced, thought, then sighed as he clapped a hand to the back of his head.

He'd been short with her last night. And this morning. After kissing the daylights out of her yesterday. Flirting with her. Meeting her eyes, her gaze, her touch, one on one. Pulling back like that because Sophie got sick was a knee-jerk reaction to an old stimulus, and yet he couldn't help it.

Could he?

"Daddy?"

"Yes, honey. How're you feeling?"

Sophie yawned. "Better. But sleepy."

"Well, it's bedtime, so that's good." He grinned, then laid his palm against her forehead. "Cool."

"Yes."

"That means the medicine is working."

"That's good, then. I want to get better so I can search for Sally the kitty. Am I going to school tomorrow?"

He squatted low. "No. I want you to have one more day of rest, so Meredith is going to keep you at her mother's house, okay?"

Sophie's eyes widened in delight.

Rachel hung over the back of his recliner. "I want to go, too."

"You are. But then Meredith is going to take you to school."

"And Sophie gets to stay?"

"She's sick, so yes."

"I'm sick, too."

Cam grinned. "What hurts?"

Rachel swept a dramatic hand across a cool, dry brow. "Everything. And I've got a tempertcher."

Cam felt her head and decided to play along. "You don't now, but I'll recheck in the morning. And if you do come down sick, maybe we can have you spend some time at Meredith's, too. Since that's what you're after."

She peered up at him, and the twist of love in his heart felt good. They were such gifts, these two. Such a mix of the life of love he'd shared with Kristy. And despite the busyness of his days and nights, he knew God had blessed him with these girls. He'd entrusted them to him.

To both of you, actually. But then Kristy died.

Cam pushed the negativity aside. Thinking about Kristy's death got him nowhere. He'd shouldered the blame, the guilt and the responsibility, but lately it wore on him, like rain battering unpainted wood. A little was okay. Too much softened the fibers, leaving it susceptible to rot and infestation.

Kind of like his soul had felt these past five years.

He hugged Rachel, grabbed Sophie's hand, and headed up the stairs with his girls, refusing to dwell in the past. A picture faced him at the landing, the last family photo they had taken before Kristy's death. He had Sophie tucked on his lap, and Kristy held a tinier Rachel on hers, and her gaze wasn't on the camera, or the child in her arms.

It was trained on him, filled with trust and love. How sad to think that trust and affection had been misplaced.

Chapter Eleven

"Here you go." Cam's morning grin brightened an already blue-sky morning.

"Hey, girls." Meredith grabbed Sophie's hand and led the way into her mother's house. "Soph, drop your stuff on the sofa. We'll set up shop out here after breakfast. You guys hungry?"

"Dad fed us." Rachel hung back, looking glum. "I told him you'd have food, but he made us eat oatmeal."

"She hates oatmeal," added Sophie. "But I like it and I'm the sick one."

"When I get sick I'm asking for baked beans, then," Rachel spouted. "And you'll have to eat a double helping because they're high in protein and really, really good for you."

Sophie ignored her, but the hinted smile told Meredith that tweaking her sister was an oft-employed device.

Poor Cam.

She turned, caught his patience-taxed expression, and jerked her head toward the door. "You go. I've got this. And Mom's going to run Rachel over to school in an hour, so we're good."

"Thanks, Mere."

"No problem." She didn't step closer, didn't walk him to

the door, didn't do any of those cozy, quiet intimacies that might hike this into more than it was, a friend doing a favor for another friend. The fact that she *wanted* to walk him to the door and give him a lingering kiss goodbye pushed her in the opposite direction.

Chicken.

Yes.

"Rachel." When the little blonde met her eyes in the kitchen, Meredith rested her gaze on a covered plate centered on the pale oak table. "Check that out."

"Danish." Rachel breathed the word with proper seven-year-old reverence.

"With frosting." Sophie's tone followed suit.

"Only the best," Meredith sang out, laughing at their delighted expressions. Her mother came through the swinging door at the opposite end of the kitchen and smiled.

"Cam's girls, I take it."

"Yup." Meredith reached out, grabbed her mother's hand, and pulled the smaller woman forward. "Mom, this is Sophie."

Sophie reached out a calm, quiet hand that said she had control of the situation in a way most nine-year-olds wouldn't for years. Very Cam-like, despite her resemblance to her mother.

"And this is Rachel."

Rachel bounded forward, grabbed Dana in a hug, and then tipped her head back, gaze up, eyes bright, smile wide. "I tried to get sick."

"Really?" Dana smiled down into Rachel's bright blue eyes and arched a brow in question. "What happened?"

"It didn't work. I even prayed about it, but God doesn't listen all the time."

Meredith squatted low. "Sure He does. But He doesn't always answer the way we want."

"Which means He's not really listening," argued Rachel.

She frowned and pointed toward Sophie. "Sophie prayed and prayed when Mommy died, asking God to send her back. He didn't."

Sophie blushed. "I was little, Rach. I didn't understand how it works."

"How what works?" Rachel swung back, impatient. "That God doesn't listen to us? I get that part, Sophie."

Sophie's expression showed mixed emotion. Embarrassment, chagrin, confusion.

Meredith bent low. "How old were you when your mother died, honey?"

Sophie seemed reluctant to explore this topic, and while Meredith understood that, she knew some things were best brought out in the open.

"Four."

"You were little."

"Yes." Sophie shrugged one shoulder in acknowledgment.

"And you were two." She met Rachel's look of indignation, and fought down a smile.

"Almost two."

Ouch. Meredith couldn't imagine the pain Cam had gone through. The shock to his system. The days and nights of work, child care and loneliness. "Sophie, it was normal for you to pray for your mom to come back when you were four. It's hard for little ones to understand what death is. They keep waiting for their loved ones to come back. Only they can't."

"I know." Sophie nodded, but her eyes looked glum.

"But you didn't know that back then," Meredith continued. "And that had to be hard, because you prayed and prayed and God didn't send Mommy back. And that had to be a big disappointment to you."

Sophie hunched forward a little. "I just wanted Daddy to be happy. To stop crying."

"Daddy doesn't cry." Rachel pronounced that in her best know-it-all voice, but the look on Sophie's face said the two-year age difference afforded them unique experiences and memories.

"It's okay to cry when someone dies." Dana slung an arm around Sophie's shoulders. "We all do."

"Not daddies." Rachel aimed a look of surprise at Dana. "I've never seen my daddy cry."

"Because you were already in bed." Sophie moved a little farther into the crook of Dana's arm. "But I couldn't fall asleep and I would climb out of bed and sit on the top stair and watch him. And pray. Real hard."

Meredith's heart squeezed tight. She didn't dare make eye contact with her mother. They'd both tear up, and that would be an awful way to start this day. She stood, tugged Rachel toward the table, and kept her voice easy. "You did the right thing, honey. And even though God can't send people back once they've gone to heaven, He heard your prayers. He loves you. And wants you to be happy."

"Then why did He let Mommy die?"

Meredith shook her head. "I don't know. I don't have any easy answers for a smart girl like you, but I know that when bad things happen to me, knowing that God loves me...looks after me...cares about me...well, that makes it easier to get through the tough times. The hard times."

"You think He listens?"

Meredith thought back to the turns her life had taken until she smartened up. "I'm sure of it. Do you still pray, Soph?"

Sophie shrugged. "Sometimes. When someone takes me to church with them. It would be rude not to, right?"

"Absolutely." Dana softened the subject by sinking into a chair, grabbing a sweet, frosted apple Danish and taking a bite. "But my favorite place to pray is in the garden. When I'm working. It's restful, smells good, and I love the sounds of birds. Bugs. Frogs and toads."

Rachel wrinkled her face in surprise as she put a cheese-filled croissant on her plate. "You can pray outside?"

"Anywhere, actually." Dana beamed at them, and waved a hand as she rose to get a pitcher of cold milk. "I love going to church because it's fun to pray with all my friends, all the people in the town—"

Rachel and Sophie exchanged a look of disbelief.

"But I pray all week. Whenever I want. I never—" she met each girl's gaze individually "—wait for church to pray. I mean, really…if God is everywhere, all the time, why in Sam Hill would I wait 'til Sunday if I feel like praying on Tuesday?"

Acceptance brightened Sophie's face. "That makes sense."

"Of course it does." Dana flashed her a grin of understanding and Meredith felt like Sophie was verging on becoming part of the sisterhood of girls everywhere, that talking things out, chatting them up, was a universal skill. "When you're playing soccer and see a clean shot, do you take it or pass the ball?"

"Take it."

"Exactly." Dana sat back down, pleased. "Carpe diem. Seize the day, the moment. Sometimes it's right to pass the ball, throw your opponent offtrack."

Both girls nodded.

"And other times—" Dana leaned in, knowing "—ya just gotta take the shot."

Meredith sat back. Seeing her mother in action with the two girls, she remembered her mother's common sense initiatives from back in the day, but she recalled something else, too.

Her anger and stubbornness had blocked her mother's efforts, like a well-practiced sweeper in a soccer game. She'd dodged and parried her mother's attempts at normalcy, even after her father had left them.

And she'd brushed off her father's death like it was just another day, ignoring his funeral.

Shame knifed her, but alongside the shame of unforgiveness was a growing awareness that she was becoming a nicer person. More giving. And more forgiving.

More like her mother.

The thought unfurled a sweet feeling within, like a little girl sprouting her wings, flying free at last. And it felt good. Real good.

Cam stopped by his mother's on the way to Meredith's that afternoon. The building inspector had given a seal of approval to the upgrades on the school-owned house and Cam had been able to list the refurbished home for sale with local Realtor Mary Kay Hammond moments ago. This was his third completed house project for the school, and he felt the success of that to his toes.

He'd worked hard to sell the original idea to the school board and the community, so he and the kids had labored strenuously on that first house. The second one had been more relaxed. This one? A piece of cake. People trusted his instinct with the kids, the homes, the sale and value prospects. And he had his eye on a new property for next year's class to start, a two-story business on Main Street caught up in a family squabble for nearly twenty years. The storefront had just come available, and the blend of residential and commercial in one property offered a one-of-a-kind learning experience for the student workers, to design a commercially attractive store at street level and twin apartments overhead.

The neglected property provided a different kind of prospect and their efforts would change an eyesore into an asset for the community.

He pulled into his mother's drive, parked and walked toward the back door, wishing for more hours in a day. Her yard needed work, her paint was starting to peel, and the roof, well…she needed a new one, but his mother wasn't one to do things ahead of time. Maybe that's why he felt a constant need to be two steps ahead of the game in all other areas of his life. Plan it, do it, move on. Although he'd neglected to find that lost, lonely kitten, and the sorrow in Sophie's eyes weighed on him. Right now, he'd give anything for more time.

"Mom?"

Quiet answered him, and while that could be construed as a good thing considering his mother's attitude, this quiet seemed wrong. No TV. No radio. No phone yakking. Just... silence.

He rounded the corner of the living, half afraid to make that last step. What if?

Don't go there.

"Mom?" He moved into the shade-darkened room. As his eyes adjusted to the dim light, he saw her sitting in the recliner, watching him. Waiting for him. But her look...her face...

Intuition pushed him forward and he crouched by her chair. Today she wasn't acting or putting on airs for the girls' benefit. This time, something was wrong. Really wrong. "Mom, what's going on? What's happened? Are you okay?"

She blinked her gaze left, thinned her lips, then brought it back to his, reluctant to let him see the sheen of tears. That bowled him over inside. Evelyn Calhoun never cried. She grumped, scolded, bothered and harangued, but crying?

Wasn't done.

He had no clue what to do. No one ever hugged his mother. Her testiness and attitude kept most people at bay, and the few friends she had were equally miserable, which meant their bad attitudes compounded one another, but now, right now, she looked like she needed a hug. So he bent low and gave her one.

She burst into tears. Not loud ones. Quiet ones. And that was worse, because quiet tears were always more serious than the noisy variety. He'd learned that with the girls. "Hey, now. Hey. What is it? What's wrong?"

He grabbed a handful of tissues from the ever-present box, and handed her a mitt full.

"Cancer."

The single word shook him. "Where?"

She pointed to her throat. "Here. Laryngeal."

"Oh, Mom." He hugged her again, not sure what to do. How to help. He released her for a minute and pulled up a kitchen chair, then grasped her hand. "What's our first step?"

She glanced away again, then shrugged. "I think I've done the first five, actually."

"Without telling anyone?" Cam sat back in disbelief. "You knew and you didn't tell us?"

She didn't follow with her normal in-your-face mode and that spiked Cam's worry. "I figured if it was nothing, there was nothing to tell. So I found out today that it's stage two and I need radiation therapy."

"Surgery, too?"

She shook her head too quickly. "No."

Fear of needles and anesthesia were just two of his mother's minor neuroses. Cam moved closer. "Before we do anything, I'm checking this out. Thoroughly."

She scowled instantly. "Which is why I kept it to myself. It's my business and I don't need a know-it-all son to come in and tell me what to do."

He met her frown with calm concern. "Too bad. That's just what's going to happen. It's only common sense these days to get second opinions, to check out all the available treatments and options, then make a decision."

"People been gettin' this cancer for a long time, and been treated the same way. They'll burn it with radiation and then watch me to see if it comes back. They already looked all through me and couldn't find anything else. Right there is something to be happy for."

She didn't look happy. She looked scared. And angry. And Cam understood that, but he also knew his mother's limitations. In her old-world view, all doctors were to be believed and respected. She didn't have internet access, she'd never choose to watch informative or educational TV, and she deliberately limited her life to her home with rare excursions out. The words *cutting-edge treatment* meant nothing to her.

And yeah, she was grumpy, opinionated and know-it-all, but she was still his mother. That tipped the scales. "When did you schedule your first treatment?"

"I haven't yet. I'm calling tomorrow."

"Good. That gives me tonight to check things out. Study up on this."

"You think you know more than doctors who spent ten years in school?" She angled him a tight look that was more than a little insulting, but Cam chalked it up to fear and normal snippiness. Belittling others had become his mother's custom a long time ago. And while he wished she were different, he'd learned to adopt the Serenity Prayer's sage reasoning. He'd change what he could and not waste time worrying about the rest. "Not more, but there are options breaking on the cancer front every day."

She drew herself forward. Her features went tight and tart. "If there were options, they would have told me."

Cam stood. "That's not always the case if they don't offer them here. Part of the new health care mentality is to keep business in the office, or the clinic, or the hospital. And part of our job as consumers is to study the options."

"There aren't any."

"Then all I'll waste is a little time," Cam told her lightly. "And because you're my mother, you're more than worth it." He bent and hugged her again, then kissed her cheek and tried but failed to recall the last time he'd kissed her. "I'll check things out and get back to you tomorrow. Do you need anything?"

"No." The sharp, single-word answer shut him out, but that wasn't unusual.

"Okay." He headed for the door, not expecting thanks or gratitude for his interference. That wasn't likely to happen, but if there were other possible treatments available, he needed to find them. He'd examine the internet later, once the girls were asleep. He didn't want them bending over his shoulder, watching as he searched cancer websites. He'd tell them in good time. But not today.

His phone buzzed as he climbed into the car.

Meredith.

His heart stretched a little wider when he spotted her name. And did he answer her call a little quicker than most?

Yes.

No.

Yes. To get it over with and move on.

That last wasn't true, but pretending not to care was the best he could do right now. "Hey. What's up? Is Sophie okay?"

"She's fine. Rachel's fine. And they'd like to do an Irish dance workout with Heather and me tonight, if that's okay. No soccer, right?"

Irish dancing? His girls? Not likely. And anyway... "They've got 4-H. If Sophie's up to it."

Meredith laughed lightly. "She heard you. I've got you on speakerphone, so their faces just fell to their toes, but I'll grab them to practice another night if that's okay."

It wasn't okay, but he wouldn't say that now, with the girls listening. They were already over-involved, but developing strong soccer skills and athletic endurance meant practice. Drills. Time. Equipment.

Dancing?

Kristy would have thought that was for sissies, and just because she wasn't here to raise her daughters, didn't mean he should disregard what she'd have done.

You have no idea what she would have done. And she's not here. You're being a schmo.

Maybe, but they were his kids. His girls. And his mother's

news put him between a rock and a hard place anyway. "I'll be there in five minutes, okay?"

"Mom made a pot of sauce. If you guys don't have supper plans, eat here, then take the girls to their meeting."

Eat with Meredith? Like a cozy family? He wanted to, therefore he couldn't. "I—"

"You'll break my mother's heart if you say no," she warned.

His inner war ended. "I can't do that. I like your mother. She's great."

"Thank you, Cameron." Dana caroled out the words, obviously pleased. And listening.

He grinned in spite of himself. "And she's right there in the room with you guys."

"Bingo. Speakerphones are marvelous things."

Meredith was on her way out when she saw Cam pull into the drive. He frowned, glanced around and raised a hand to pause her. "Where are you going?"

"Stillwaters. I told you, Heather and I are doing a workout."

"Before dinner?"

She softened her voice as if speaking to a small child. "Big girls can warm up food later if they want to. I have a microwave. And I need to check on the bathroom tear outs, and figure my game plan for this week. If you could stop by later tomorrow and make sure the bathroom remodel won't break historic code, I'd be grateful. These guys aren't quite as sensitive to the landmark status as they should be, and I don't want an unnecessary delay."

"Will do. So." He shifted a look of disappointment from her car to the house and back. "You're really going?"

His look nearly undid her, but she'd read the hesitation in his voice when she invited him to stay and eat. She'd heard the reluctance. Removing herself made it easier all around. "Yes. Duty calls. But you'll have fun with Mom and the girls, and the sauce is amazing. And she's got garlic bread, too, done on artisan bread from Bread-n-Bagel."

"That store's addictive."

Meredith laughed as she walked to her car. "It is. And it's only one of the reasons I'm working out with Heather. That and Megan's cookie store. Their candy shop. Too many reasons to eat wrong, each more delightful than the next."

"See ya."

He looked woebegone as she did a K-turn in the drive, and his lost-puppy look wasn't lost on her.

But she'd be silly to stay. Selfish to hope. Crazy to dream when she knew what her past could do to her present, so she flashed him a bright smile and headed away from the great-smelling sauce and perfectly cooked pasta. Mouth-watering good, but then so was Cam Calhoun and the less they were together, the easier things would be.

So ten minutes later when she saw the gouge the plumbers had left on the formerly flawless dining room floor, she was ready to duke it out with the next available person. Unfortunately, Heather walked in at that moment.

"Uh-oh." She crossed the room, saw the mark and scowled. "The bathroom guys did this?"

"That's my take. They were the only ones here today."

Heather snatched up her phone. "You want to call them or shall I?"

"Have at it." Heather's instant indignation reminded Meredith she had a partner now. A friend. A colleague. And that she didn't have to do everything alone. Not in business, anyway.

She listened as Heather talked to the owner of the kitchen and bath remodeling store, then remembered another good thing about small towns.

Everyone had everyone's private number.

That made her grin and sigh. Sometimes privacy was a good thing. But in this case? She gave Heather and the phone an admiring look once the call was disconnected. "He's coming over?"

"Right now."

"I'm impressed. Beyond impressed. We'll go right to—"

Heather shrugged her off, and drew out a magazine layout for her to see. "He used to be the only game in town, but now that Jamison and Wellsville are on the rebound, he's got competition. Other contractors are advertising here, supporting local sports teams, coming to fairs and festivals. If he wants our business, he needs to make good on this. That's a century-and-a-quarter-old hardwood floor there, and if we let this go, who knows how careless those guys will get?"

"My thoughts exactly." Meredith slung an arm around her shoulders. "Have I mentioned how glad I am to have you on board?"

"Remember that tomorrow when Mrs. Dennehy comes in to get her hair cut."

"My smile-and-nod reflex is ready. And Grandma's coming in tomorrow, so that will take the edge off."

"Perfect." Heather tapped a finger on the furniture page she'd marked, the cozy-looking, oversize high-quality sectional flanking a conversation area. "What do you think of this layout for the spa waiting room upstairs?"

"Love it." Meredith hiked both brows in appreciation. "Earth tones, warmth, soft light, great feel to the whole thing. And probably out of our price range."

"It's not. Haley Jennings has a connection."

"The woman doing the cooperative near the interstate?"

Heather nodded. "Her neighbor is a friend of Rory's. She fell on some hard times and I helped her out, so Haley told me she'd get us anything we needed at cost. They're planning a small furniture store in the new cooperative, and she's got a contract with them already."

Meredith eyed the price tag and whistled. "That saves us nearly two thousand dollars."

"And another five hundred on the lighting."

"Seriously?"

Heather deadpanned a dramatic look. "Oh, honey. When comes to money, I am never anything but serious. Life has way of doing that to you."

Meredith knew that, but she'd made great money these past ive years. She might have forgotten that bottom-line pricing vas huge, and being a businesswoman she couldn't afford o forget that now. "This is awesome, Heather. Thank you."

Heather grinned as a knock sounded at the side door. "And nat is most likely our bathroom-remodeling friend, hopefully eady to make things right. Okay if I take the lead?"

It was more than okay. It bordered on wonderful to share ne responsibility with a trusted friend. "Go for it. I'll listen nd learn."

Heather smiled, welcomed the shop owner in, and within ive minutes had his promise of repair and a cool two-undred-and-fifty-dollar reduction in the overall cost. And pledge that his workers would treat the gracious old home nore politely in the future.

"Cam will be upset," Meredith told Heather as they headed pstairs thirty minutes later.

"Why?"

"Because I was home with Sophie today. She was sick. nd if I'd been here, they'd have been more careful."

"True." Heather acknowledged that with a nod and a shrug. But good contractors do their best whether the owner is on-ite or not. So now we've got the owner involved. And he oesn't want to lose money, so I expect his people will be nore careful. But how *interesting*—" she rolled out the words s she shrugged off her sweatshirt and kicked off her street hoes "—that you were babysitting Cam Calhoun's little girl. 'are to say more?"

"No."

"Don't have to, anyway." Heather stretched. "I already

knew that. Shoot, probably half the town knows it becaus
Jody Gransby saw you and Sophie sitting on the porch thi
afternoon, reading."

"And she just happened to mention it to…?"

"A neighbor who shall go unnamed, who then calle
Megan Romesser at home, who said it wasn't polite to gos
sip and hung up."

"Then called you."

Heather grinned, smug. "Of course. Because she reall
wanted to know the scoop."

Meredith saw two choices: laugh or cry. She decide
to laugh and shook her head as she joined Heather in th
stretches. "I never even thought of that. Of what people woul
think with Cam dropping the girls off. Sitting out there. I'v
been gone too long, it seems."

"Well, who cares what anyone thinks?" Heather wondere
out loud. "We might not be able to change our proximity t
people, but we can change how we let it affect us. And sinc
the majority of people in our town are nice—"

"True."

"—we ignore the rest and deal with them as needed. N
sense borrowing trouble. Oh, there's Rory," she added as th
downstairs door swung shut. "She's going to work out wit
us tonight."

"Didn't she just finish her lesson?"

Heather nodded. "She's determined. She wants a career o
stage at some point. And yes, I've tried to discourage her te
ways to Sunday, but she thinks she's got what it takes and
can't disagree. But what a hard life. Always waiting on tha
next call. The next gig. Being part of a troupe."

"Or being a headliner and center stage." Rory's optimis
tic interruption drew Meredith's smile and Heather's grin.

"That's my girl. Dream big."

"And work hard."

"Amen." Meredith turned on the music and looked left. "Ready?"

"I am."

"Yes." Rory shrugged out of her fleece, twirled and assumed a takeoff position perfectly.

"Show-off."

She grinned at Meredith and splayed her fingers as if reaching to catch the notes, hinting at the woman within. Strong. Assertive. Charming. Ambitious. Industrious. And a stunning talent, to boot.

She'd need every bit of it to make it on the stage, but how wonderful to have that dream and carry it through. Seeing Rory here, ready to work more, drove the point home. Hard work and goal-setting were their own education, and nothing to be shrugged off. All the fancy degrees in the world got you nowhere without a strong work ethic. How blessed she was to be surrounded by that at last.

Chapter Twelve

Cam pulled into his mother's drive early the next morning, armed for battle. One light glowed in the kitchen. His mother wasn't a fan of high electric bills so she was probably up and sequestered near the coffeepot. He knocked and waited for her to open the door. She expected him late in the day. Early morning?

Not so much.

"Cameron." She opened the door and settled her features into a thin, grim line. "You came over to order me around."

"Yup." He bent and kissed her cheek. He'd decided yesterday that not kissing his mother was wrong. Not hugging his mother was worse. And not showing love and affection was a bad habit, so he was determined to stop the downward trend now. "Have a seat while I grab coffee."

"Don't you have to be at school?"

"My first class isn't until nine-oh-five, and I called the principal and told her I was running late. So…" He spread out several internet printouts for his mother's perusal. "Here you go."

"I told you I don't need help or advice." She tapped a thick finger against the paper, her nails bitten to the quick, and tha told Cam she'd started biting them again, a habit she'd stopped long ago. Unless she was nervous. Or depressed. Or scared.

He'd go with all three.

"And I didn't listen, which is a good thing," he continued as he pushed one paper in front of her. "Look at this."

"What is it?"

He sent her an overused look of patience. She sighed out loud and read, then shook her head. "This says I don't need no radiation."

"Correct."

"But how?"

"Laser surgery." Cam took his pencil from his breast pocket and circled the doctor's location. "And his practice is right up in Rochester. He's with the University of Rochester Medical Center and he's an expert in laryngeal cancer."

"But—"

"No buts." Cam leaned closer. "This is like a miracle, Mom. It's doable. There are only a few of these doctors in the entire country right now, it's that new, but this one is right here. And there was a video of a guy who'd had the surgery, and he talked about his quick recovery. How he went right back to work, and he's had no recurrence. It would be silly of us not to check this out."

"I can't drive to Rochester. That's two hours."

Cam smiled and laid a hand on her shoulder. "But I can. And there are plenty of people around to watch the girls."

"Like Meredith Brennan."

He refused to get into this now. "Like Meredith, yes. The girls love her. And she's very good with them."

"She'll fill their heads with all sorts of nonsense. That's been her way from the beginning. And then she'll up and leave the minute the going gets tough."

"We're not discussing Meredith," Cam told her. He firmed his voice to drive the point. "We're focusing on your health. Your well-being. Your life."

"So you can boss me around, but I'm not supposed to have a say about what you do? Who you see?"

He stood, grinned and hugged her. "Got it. We understand each other perfectly. I'm going to help take care of you. But you've got to let me live my own life, my way. Deal?"

A hint of a smile almost graced her mouth. And that hint was enough to tell Cam that she appreciated his efforts. He waved the paper in front of her. "Do you want to call and make the appointment or shall I?"

"I haven't said yes."

"And I won't take 'no' for an answer, so we're deadlocked. But I'm bigger and stronger."

"I'll call. I'll see what they say. And that's all I want to hear about it."

He gave her one last hug and felt her hug him back, a rarity in the Calhoun house. "Let me know what they say later, okay? I'll come by before I start work at the spa."

"Spas. Facials. Manicures." She hid her hands, probably remembering what she'd done to her nails. "Bah."

"See you later."

She didn't answer, but she did walk him to the door, and he thought her step and her posture looked a little brighter. A little stronger. And that was a great beginning.

Claire Dennehy drew deliberate attention as she hobbled through Heather's door midmorning. Her exaggerated huffing added sound to the visual drama.

Heather hurried over and took her arm. Her action shamed Meredith, because no matter what Claire had done, who she'd hurt, she was still an aged woman in need of assistance. God would expect her to bury the hatchet and offer a hand, the whole seventy-times-seven thing. About that? She was a work in progress. Slow progress, besides. Therefore she needed to try harder. "Claire, good morning. That wind is brisk today, isn't it?"

"We need the wind to dry up all that rain," the older woman barked.

Heather paused.

The customer in Heather's chair froze in place, a hand raised midair.

Resolute, Meredith smiled and nodded as she applied curl refiner to her grandmother's hair, both moves well-practiced. "It should help."

"Will help, you mean." Claire advanced two steps, close enough for Meredith to feel the temperature rise around her. Obviously the expression "steaming mad" had some basis in fact. "And I don't appreciate people yelling at my friends, young lady. Being disrespectful to your elders is what leads to trouble, and I'd have thought you had enough trouble with folks to last a lifetime when you were here before, but I guess I was wrong."

"Claire." Heather tried to intervene, but Meredith raised a calming hand in her direction.

"Let her have her say."

"And I will, too." Claire thumped her cane against the floor. "Evelyn Calhoun is a good woman who's done nothing but work hard all her life. She doesn't deserve to be dressed down by someone who comes back from the city all fancied up. And while we're at it, what brought you back, Meredith Brennan? Because we know you hated these towns, the people, bein' home. So."

She peered closer and Meredith saw the tiny look of triumph in the sour old woman's eyes, as if cornering prey made her feel good. How sad.

"Why did you come back?" Claire drawled the words as if interrogating her.

Meredith could have returned the shots with ease. She might have argued her point and won. She could have parried the elderly woman's thrusts and dodged her blows, but what fun was there in that? She leaned in, spiked a grin and said, "To nab Cam Calhoun and those precious girls. Why else?"

Heather choked. Her customer snorted, laughing.

Claire rounded her shoulders, and Meredith went back to styling her grandmother's hair, but Helen Walker wasn't about to stand down.

Uh-oh.

Helen didn't let the raised adjustable chair stop her. With a single bound she popped out of the seat. Her posture and the sharp intelligence in her bright brown eyes exemplified her CEO-like presence. "Who do you think you are, Claire Dennehy?"

"I…um…"

"You didn't notice me sitting in the chair, did you? You thought it was okay to walk in here and go off on my granddaughter because of something that happened fourteen years ago."

"Helen, I—"

"Don't try to explain. Don't try to make this right. Don't try to make excuses when you've done nothing but give this girl grief since puberty."

Meredith wanted to break up the face-off, but she didn't dare. When Grandma got on a roll, the best option was to get out of the way. And that's exactly what Meredith did. Besides, it was kind of fun to see Grandma stand up for her. Watch Claire back down. Fun in a very naughty way, of course.

But still fun.

"My granddaughter is a beautiful, accomplished young woman. She was drummed out of town by senseless gossip back then, and there is no way I'm letting that same thing happen again," Helen stormed. "She is bringing her art and expertise to an area that really needs it. She's got a great partner." Grandma noted Heather with her gaze. "She also has financial backing and an opportunity for more jobs in the area. And if Cam Calhoun has any good sense about him, he'll drop down on bended knee and propose before any one of half a dozen fine men win her hand because that's—" Meredith nearly choked on that, but held her own as Grandma leaned closer to Claire "—how…" Helen drew closer yet, her art of intimidation showcasing CEO to the max. "Amazing she is. And now an apology would be in order, and quickly, too. I have a meeting at ten and you've messed up my blow-dry."

"Grandma, I—"

Helen shot her an arch look that said "hush."

Claire turned, haughty, but slightly penitent. "I apologize if I was out of line."

"If?" Helen's face said there was no question.

Claire frowned, glowered, then sighed. "I was out of line. When I heard how she sassed Evelyn Calhoun at the Easter egg hunt, I went a little crazy. Evelyn is my friend."

"Regardless." Helen faced her firm. "Too much talk and scuttlebutt has gone on at my family's expense. Yes, my son-in-law was a criminal. A womanizer. A drinker and addict, besides. That's common knowledge. But why anyone would think it's okay to target people who are already emotionally hurting, is beyond me. It stops now."

Claire's strong features faltered. She inhaled, glanced around, then lowered her chin. "You're right, Helen. On all counts. I get defensive over Evelyn, her being alone and all."

"Her choice." Helen's tone said she'd cut the old women no slack.

Claire didn't disagree. She turned toward Meredith and stuck her hand out. "I do apologize. I didn't used to be so hard and harsh."

Meredith couldn't agree with that, but maybe the woman was thinking back more decades than Meredith could recall. "Thank you, Claire. And what I said about Cam?"

Claire nodded and shrugged, embarrassed. "You were kidding. I know."

Meredith lowered her chair for Helen to resume her seat

and sent Claire a quick, knowing grin as her grandmother resettled. "Maybe not."

Helen looked up and winked in approval.

Cam's heavy footfall announced his arrival at the spa that evening. "You've got designs on me, I hear."

"You heard that already?" Meredith glanced up at him from her spot on the floor in the upstairs hall and made a face. "Impressive."

She sat back, scrutinized the sponge effect, waggled her head to show indecision, then stood. "I said that to quiet down a bothersome old bird. And then my grandmother jumped in and went to bat for me. Word of warning—don't make my grandmother mad."

"Wouldn't dream of it." He studied the splotched wall. "I liked it better plain."

"I agree." She met his gaze, then pursed her lips. "Which means I just wasted two hours."

"Experiential learning." He came forward, hooked his thumbs in his pockets, and shoulder-bumped her. "Common practice in my trade."

"I thought you employed the measure-twice, cut-once theory."

"Doesn't work in all applications. Like this." He smiled toward the messed-up wall. "Sometimes you just gotta get in there, try it and see."

"No biggie, in any case." She recapped the dusky tan paint cap and tossed the sponge into the oversize utility garbage bag. "Nothing another shot with the roller won't cure."

"Exactly. So." He moved closer and hooked a thumb beneath her chin to hold her gaze. "Did you mean it?"

"No. Of course not." She tried to step away but he slipped the other arm around her waist, holding her in place, and the feel of his arm, the look in his eyes, the slight curve of his mouth…

Suddenly she didn't want to get away at all.

"Truth." His thumb stroked the soft underside of her chin. A lazy smile tugged his mouth. "You got your cap set for me, Miss Brennan?"

She'd love to be able to set her cap for him. She'd figured that out when she first laid eyes on him, all studious and stern. Rugged and strong. With his cute, rimless glasses. And she'd toss in her shoes, purse and any other accessory she could find, but he didn't know her past.

She did. She smiled lightly and touched his nose with her index finger. "I do not. But if you're available, I'll put the word out."

"You sure?" He drew her closer, his words tempting her heart while his breath tickled her skin. His lips followed the whispered words and he nuzzled the softness of her cheek with the gentlest of kisses. "Because I might just like it if you did."

"But—"

The kiss swallowed her protest. Cam gathered her in, and his mouth, his lips staked a claim she didn't dare allow.

But her heart beat faster. And the muscles she worked so hard to keep toned went soft. Breathing became nonessential, because the only thing she needed right then and there was to kiss him back, like it was the most natural thing in the world to be in Cam's arms again. Kissing him. Thinking of him. Dreaming about him.

"Cam."

"Shush."

He kissed her again, and in Cam's head everything that had been wrong with his world seemed right again. The feel of Meredith in his arms, the scent of her skin, coffee, paint and spiced vanilla, the sight of her working on this old place he loved, day after day, in speckled sweats and bandannas.

She was the same, but different. Still bold and beautiful,

but unafraid to get down and dirty as the job required. He loved that about her.

He loved her.

He paused the kiss, reality pushing him back. He couldn't love Meredith.

But he did.

Caution warred with desire. He had the girls to consider.

They were already smitten with her.

She'd run before. She might run again. And then where would he be with two brokenhearted kids? He stepped back, determined to take this slow. One look at her upturned face, those long, dark eyelashes, a gorgeous mouth just meant for kissing…

Time to put the brakes on. Past time, actually. Except he didn't want to, but that might be old-fashioned lust and loneliness. He hadn't dated since he lost Kristy. And didn't Meredith deserve someone who would look out for her? Care for her? He'd messed up before, caught up in work, much like he was now. Even after five years of single parenthood, he wasn't sure he had what it took to be the kind of man and husband a woman needed and deserved.

"Cam." She raised a hand to his face, and her expression reflected his gut. "I can't do this."

"I know." He nodded, agreeable. "Me, either. So why do you suppose it keeps happening?" He tightened his grip at her waist and refused to fight the smile she inspired by looking so staunch and serious.

"Because we're lonely and we're caught together on a work project."

"In a romantic old house that I've loved for years."

"And we've got a history," she went on.

"That ended badly," he agreed.

"So, naturally, we wonder." She glanced at his mouth, then away, guilty.

"And think…." He assumed a more serious expression. "Maybe dream."

"You dream of me, Cam?" Her voice went whisper soft, as if those two little words meant the world to her. Did he dare admit it? One look at her longing gaze said yes.

"Constantly. It's quite annoying, actually. And then there's this." He laid one quick, sweet kiss to her mouth before he stepped back. "Which I thoroughly enjoy, by the way, but we both keep backtracking and frankly, Mere, I can't afford to mess up. Not the job, not the life." He waved his hand from her back to him. "We're working together. And that's nice. And yeah, I'd like it to be more, but I can't make mistakes. Take chances. I needed this job to pay for Sophie's braces. And I need the next job to get through summer. And then I teach to pay the bills, because raising kids is no walk in the park. And if I fall in love with you and it doesn't work out, then I've messed up two little girls who mean the world to me, and I can't do that. Correction." He splayed his hands. "I can't live with myself if I do that. So I don't mess around. I don't date. I don't take chances that might break my girls' hearts. Because they mean everything to me."

Meredith's head nodded agreement, but her eyes…

Oh, those eyes…

They held shadows. Sorrow. Guilt. Cam had no trouble reading the emotions because they reflected his feelings too well, and that made him wonder why she'd feel that way.

Fourteen years. A lot could happen to a person in fourteen years. He knew that. He'd lived it.

"Let's take it slow." He bent closer, wishing he didn't have to apply the brakes at all.

"Or stop," Meredith suggested. She met his gaze quietly. "That's probably the better option, Cam."

He grinned and turned for the stairs. "Not when I like kissing you so much, Mere. But I can't kiss you if I'm on the first floor and you're up here repainting that horrible excuse for a wall."

"Hey."

"Hey, yourself." He turned and blinked, long and slow. "I'll be around."

Her tentative smile made him long to stay. But two promising athletes needed him to be strong. Careful. Cautious. Even when that was the last thing he wanted to be.

Hormones aside, those girls were worth every bit of caution life entailed. He'd let them down once, big-time. He'd never do it again.

Chapter Thirteen

Good Friday, thought Cam as he went to stow his laptop in the carry case. That meant Easter was two days away. And he'd done nothing to prepare for the day. No candy for a basket. No pretty new clothes for the girls. No fancy bonnets. No thought of gathering in a church, surrounded by other well-dressed kids.

Who needed all that stuff, anyway?

He scowled at the internet reminder, hollered for the girls one more time, then glared at the clock. He could run by the candy shop later, but experience told him every other last-minute shopper would crowd Grandma Mary's candies late in the day because the candy store closed from noon to three on Good Friday.

In an old-fashioned town, old ideas clung tight.

With school off for the day, he'd scheduled an efficient time frame for the spa's built-in cabinets. And he knew Meredith was working at Heather's today and tomorrow. Heather's business had boomed since Meredith came on board, and with Easter upon them, everyone in town would look good.

Except the Calhoun girls.

He'd messed up again, he knew it, but how could he fix things and keep his commitments for the morning? He'd promised Meredith he'd work at the spa while the plumbing crew continued their progress on the main-floor restrooms and the upstairs spa shower room. She'd hoped his presence would inspire added care on their part. And the furnace guy was supposed to meet him at eleven, so that left no wiggle room to get over to the candy store.

And the girls would be with him all day tomorrow, messing up any chance of surprise.

Rachel pounded down the stairs, ready for a day at the Grishams' house. Sophie followed in her more sedate fashion, a clutch of books in one hand, her bag slung over the other shoulder. "Better check her stuff," she announced as she reached the first floor, jerking her head Rachel's way. "She was on the computer while we were supposed to be getting ready."

"Without my permission?" Cam frowned and bent low. "You know that's not allowed, right?"

Rachel bit her lip, sent Sophie an "I'll getcha later" look, and shrugged. "Yes."

"So why did you do it?"

She raised her shoulders again and thrust out her bottom lip. "I don't know."

"Rachel, I have to be able to trust you, even when I can't see you. Especially when I can't see you." Cam paused. He hated what he was about to say, but said it anyway, seeing no choice. "No TV today. Or treats. You can't keep ignoring the rules and doing things your way. You're the kid. I'm the grown-up. That puts me in charge. Like it or not."

She didn't like it one little bit, that was plain to see, but to her credit she didn't cry or come undone. Neither did she scream, shout or berate him. She took the punishment like a true soldier, and that almost made him second-guess his edict, but one of them had to be tough. Strong. Set rules for safety and decorum.

"Did you both put your breakfast dishes in the sink?"

Sophie nodded.

Rachel gulped.

"Go. Do it." Cam pointed toward the back door. "Then hop in the car, get belted and I'll drop you off down the road."

"Okay." Rachel walked stoop-shouldered and guilt-riddled, her shuffling step pleading for mercy.

Not gonna happen. Kids needed to follow directions. Behave. Be respectful.

A niggle of guilt made him wonder why she'd hopped on the upstairs computer. Rachel wasn't inclined toward computer games; she could care less about kids' clubs on the web, and she'd never requested one of those hand-held systems. So why would she break the rules and use his desktop?

He almost went up to check, but the clock nagged him out the door. He couldn't afford to waste any of a precious day off when he hoped to turn the corner of accomplishment at the spa.

Meredith had put in a whirlwind morning at Heather's, and a glance at the time said there wasn't time to go home and change before the Good Friday afternoon service. A cold front ushered in a driving April storm. The rain beat down, relentless, the leaden sky and naked trees enough to make her wonder if spring would ever truly come. She hit Cam's number and jumped in when he answered, no preliminaries. "Hey, it's me, I was wondering if you'd like me to pick the girls up and take them to church with me."

Silence met her offer and for a quick second she wondered if she'd lost the call, but then Cam hummed a light *Hmm,* a habit she remembered as if high school were yesterday.

Which it wasn't.

"Thanks, but no. They're at the Grishams' for the day, having fun with their girls. I wouldn't want to interrupt that and it would be rude to ask them and not take the Grisham kids."

"Or take them all," Meredith suggested. She didn't know

Mrs. Grisham, but Tony had been a year ahead of her in school. Would it seem weird to stop by and see if the girls wanted to go? Probably. And Cam's reaction? Not wanting to interrupt their fun for God? For Christ? For Good Friday?

That was sad beyond words.

"You're right," she went on, gliding over his missed opportunity to figure out this whole God relationship thing. "Gotta go. I'm coming over after services. I want to begin work on that first spa room upstairs and Heather's coming by later for a workout."

"All right."

He was either prickly or busy or both. And maybe she'd touched a nerve by offering to take the girls, but hadn't he said they'd gone to church with friends before? So maybe it was her. Or the rush of feelings swirling around them. Cozying up to the girls probably seemed like backdoor politics, and she'd seen enough of that to last a lifetime.

She headed to Jamison, determined to spend at least part of this afternoon with God. Just God. The service at the White Church at the Bend was in its opening minutes as she stepped into the old building.

Soft yellow light warmed the dark day. And while her brother Matt's quick patch job at Thanksgiving had stopped the roof from actually leaking into the sanctuary, the yellowed ceiling spots and scent of mildew said the aged structure needed help. Help she hoped would be forthcoming between her family's largesse and their skilled workmanship.

Katie Bascomb plunked soft notes on her violin. The violin was more fiddle than anything else most Sundays, but today Katie coaxed sad, drawn-out notes from the polished instrument. Their poignancy drifted on damp air, the heating system not quite enough to dry the dankness in the ceiling. The roof. The walls.

And suddenly Meredith was glad she wasn't attending service in some perfect church. Some pristine palace of prayer.

Because the tired holes in her soul felt at home here, in this battered house of God.

She had done the right thing by coming home. Putting old demons to rest. Starting fresh, beginning anew.

And it felt good. Oh, so good. She slipped into a seat alongside Maude McGinnity, a Jamison old-timer. Maude reached out and clasped her hand in welcome, a signal of hope. Camaraderie.

As Katie's notes waned, Pastor Si raised his hands high. He wasn't wearing his famous Louisiana football jersey today, but he wasn't decked out in vestments, either. Not Si. He sported black pants and a long-sleeved T-shirt that read, "Preach the Gospel at all times. When all else fails, use words."

The old quote made Meredith smile and cringe. *Live your faith.* That's what the words meant. Set an example by what you do, not what you say.

She hadn't done that for a very long time, but she could. She knew she could.

"Father, forgive them. They know not what they do." Si quoted the solemn entreaty in a strained voice, emulating the sorrow and pain of crucifixion.

Meredith's heart stretched wider, recognizing her personal weakness. Forgiveness. Tough gig. Easy in word, so hard in deed. And forgetting those wrongs?

Impossible.

His words touched her. He and his brother had lost their parents in the terror attacks on the World Trade Center years ago. Once in a while he talked about the ensuing lapse of faith and trust that had followed those heinous times.

But he'd turned things around, despite his loss.

And so could she. Yes, she'd sinned. She'd lived a life some would consider normal for this day and time, but Meredith was beyond fooling herself. Prettying up behavior with excuses was a thing of the past.

Accepting it? Moving on?

That was the here and now.

She saw Maude home. The driving rain made surfaces slippery, and Maude seemed to favor her left hip.

"I'm fine," Maude insisted as Meredith put a gentle grip on her arm for the outside stairs.

"I know that." Meredith grinned at her. "But I'm putting Si's words into practice. You were listening, right?"

Maude smiled back. "He's got a way about him, doesn't he?"

"Yes." He did. Simon's simple, matter-of-fact preaching felt good. Simple and direct. She liked that. "And he's way cute."

"Cuter than Cameron Calhoun?" The teasing glance said not much got by Maude. Or the rest of the town, for that matter.

Meredith shrugged one shoulder. "No one's cuter than Cam."

"I thought as much." Maude turned the door handle to the quilt shop, let herself in, then smiled at Meredith's surprise. "I never lock the door on Good Friday. Overnight, yes. Today, no."

"Brave."

"Or foolhardy, but for that little space of time." Maude directed her gaze toward the circle of churches, visible through the colonial-style window on her right. "I like to think the world's a nice, normal place again, where folks respect what others have and work for their own."

Meredith gave her an impromptu hug. "I love that idea."

Maude hugged her back. "An old woman's ramblings. You have a good day, now, and thank you for seeing me home. But you're going to be soaked going back to your car."

"It's just rain. And I'm going straight home to get changed because I'm painting a spa room tonight."

"I'll be one of your first customers," Maude declared. "I think I'll keep my natural salt-and-pepper shade, but a new cut-and-curl might be just the ticket!"

"And maybe a pedicure?"

Maude's smile went wide. "I've never had such a thing, Meredith."

"No time like the present to start. Half-price senior discount on the mani-pedi."

"I'll do it. And maybe make a habit of it," Maude added. "At my age, new habits are hard come by."

"Then let's change that." Meredith gave her a quick wave, then darted back into the rain.

The heavens opened. By the time she got to the car she was soaked through. She hit a button and welcomed the blast of an efficient heating system. Yes, she was cold, wet and messy. Wretchedly so.

But she felt great.

Cam called her cell nearly two hours later. She tried to tamp down the little thrill of anticipation when his number popped into the screen, but no. Her pulse skittered up and her heart smiled on its own. "Hey. What's up?"

"Are you at the spa?"

"Yes." She glanced around and said, "Which is where you said you'd be, right?"

"The storm took down a tree at the house."

"Your house?"

"No. The school's house. The one where I conduct my classes."

"Oh, Cam." He and the kids had put heart and soul into that rebuild. Their care and devotion was evidenced throughout. "Is anyone hurt?"

"No, thank God."

A tiny smile lit her heart further at his choice of words. Maybe he wasn't as hardened as he thought. "Did it hit the house?"

"Yes. Took out a front corner. I'm going to be caught up here while we do emergency enclosures and I was wondering if the girls could come over there and hang out? The Grishams will drop them off."

"Of course. I'll unlock the side door."

"They'll need to eat. I was going to grab Chinese food tonight."

"Consider it done."

"Meredith, I—"

"Oops, gotta go, Cam. My paint's drying."

It wasn't, but she refused to let him argue about buying the girls some food. Yes, she got it that he'd refused her earlier offer for whatever reasons. Fourteen years meant a lot had happened on both sides of the fence, and giving Cam space and time? She was fine with that. Mostly. Not when she was kissing him. At that point she wanted things to fast-forward with lightning speed.

But rationally, she got it. And she recognized the limitations she needed to set. There was no way to reconcile who she was and what she'd done with being a substitute mother. But she could still hang out with the girls. Chat with them.

Love them.

That emotional truth bit deep, but wasn't that exactly what Simon said today? To show our love, not just voice it. So she would, because hanging with Sophie and Rachel should never be about her, but about them.

Cam was cold, wet, tired and disappointed in the day. His well-laid plans had been waylaid by the unfortunate accident at the house, and he'd lost precious work time at the spa while overseeing the emergency repairs to shield the living room corner of the house from further damage. A local tree surgeon had removed the offending tree and the downed electric wires had been replaced by the electric company.

But he'd lost a whole day. Not good. Never good in the eyes of a guy on limited time. He'd have to work extra tomorrow to make up for it, and that only jammed his Easter weekend responsibilities tighter. Why hadn't he just ordered stuff for the girls on the internet and been done with it?

"Hey." The girls were shrugging into their jackets as he came through the porch door of the spa. He splayed his hands in apology to Meredith and Heather. "Sorry. It took a while to get the wires back up and the tree cleared out. I didn't mean to be this late and mess up your workout."

"You didn't," Heather told him. She tossed a backpack to Sophie and turned more fully toward Cam. "They worked out with us."

"Meredith and Heather taught us some Irish dancing," Rachel spouted. Delight emanated from her despite the late hour, and she did a quick step-toe move that reminded Cam of a younger Meredith. "And I can do this." Rachel rose on tiptoe, then three-stepped around the room, joyful and carefree. Sophie followed, her dark hair dancing in the light, the natural bob and weave of the step tumbling her head full of curls.

Only Sophie didn't have curls. Not in her hair's natural state.

And his girls didn't dance, worry about tights or hair bows, fancy shoes or fingernails. And yet both girls sported pink nail polish and step-toed their way around the grand old entrance as if born to it. Which they were with his Irish heritage.

And they weren't because he was their father, and he had the responsibility to point them in the right direction. And this wasn't it.

"Let's go."

"Did you like it?" Sophie came to a perfect stop before him, her face upturned, eagerly awaiting his approval.

He tugged the upper part of her jacket closed. "You did well."

"And me, too?" Rachel flashed him an imp smile, her trademark, and despite their inherent differences, it was clear that the girls' athleticism worked favorably in the dance.

"Wonderful. Now thank Meredith and Heather for a one-of-a-kind night and head to the car, okay? It's late."

"Thank you, Meredith." Sophie gave Meredith a lingering hug, then did the same with Heather, and that surprised Cam. Sophie was the more solitary daughter. And definitely not a hugger. "I had so much fun."

"Good." Meredith beamed down at her, braced herself, then wrapped Rachel's more rugged onslaught in an embrace. "You did great, kid."

"I know." Rachel grinned, and the endearing gap in her top front teeth stretched the smile that much wider. "I can't wait to learn more. Can we practice again?"

"Absolutely. Just say the word."

Cam drew a breath between tight teeth. He knew Meredith read him, read him like a book, and she'd darted a troubled glance at him as the girls showed off their new moves, but to openly promise them something against his wishes?

No way, uh-uh. "Head to the car, girls. Get buckled in. I'll be right there."

For once they did as asked, and that should have relieved him, but at this point of a wasted day, not much would do that except a solid seven hours of sleep. And then he'd do it all again. He watched the girls until he was sure they'd gotten through the second door, then swung back, determined to have his say.

He'd forgotten that Meredith preferred offense to defense. She came at him, her pretty face taut and defensive and reamed him out, big time.

"You big lug. Coming in here all bent out of shape because your day went down the tubes and then acting like that. You should be ashamed of yourself, but if you're not, I'm ashamed enough for you. What on earth were you thinking?"

"Thinking?" He leaned in, wondering just how much worse this day could get. He was about to find out. "I'm thinking you had no permission to teach my girls how to dance. Or paint their nails. Or fill their heads with all kinds of nonsense about looking good, being pretty, doing hair and any of the other nonessential life lessons you embrace, Meredith." He infringed on her space further, mad at himself for railing on her, mad at her for taking so much on herself, but then this was Meredith. She'd always stepped out in front of the crowd. But not with Sophie and Rachel. He wasn't about to allow that.

"You." She jabbed a finger into his chest, making him glad he still wore his jacket. "Are acting like a Neanderthal baboon. There is nothing wrong with Irish dancing, it's an historic art, great exercise and marvelous body discipline for sequential movement. It's as athletic as any sport in the nation, and I refuse to have you belittle me—" the finger poked again as she backed him toward the door "—my friends—" she hooked a thumb toward the kitchen, where Heather no doubt watched and listened to the whole reality-TV-type show they were putting on "—or my job. Got it?"

He planted his feet and maybe it was the texture of the day mixed with guilt over dissing God, church and his dead wife, but whatever it was, he scowled, hissed a breath and said, "They're mine. Just mine. Don't mess with them again."

Her skin paled. Her dark blue eyes hazed with hurt, then shadowed with resignation. She took a broad step back, bit her lower lip, narrowed her gaze and pointed to the door. "Get out."

He left.

It didn't matter that he'd regretted the words the instant they flew out of his mouth, or that he knew he was overreacting. At that moment, with multiple internal reactions raging, all he wanted was for the world to leave him alone to raise his daughters as he saw fit, even though he'd managed to mess up Easter. Again.

He climbed into the driver's seat and headed home, really wishing he'd invested in a punching bag. The last time he got this mad he'd left a hole in the screened porch wall. His knuckles ached, remembering that. He felt stupid, tired and downright disgusted with himself for going over the top.

The girls sent worried glances at him through the rear-view mirror.

He didn't dare say a word, or even open his mouth. He'd already done irreparable harm to a woman who meant nothing but good for his girls, and having voiced his stupid command, there was no way to fix it. Undo it.

What made him act like a first-class jerk to the woman he was falling in love with all over again?

And if he thought things couldn't possibly get worse, he was wrong. So wrong. Because once the girls were tucked into bed and the lights turned off, the glow of his desktop computer drew him into the upstairs office. He frowned, remembered that Rachel had been online that morning and strode across the room to shut it down. His movement stirred the sensors, and the screen popped up in a blaze of light, a totally feminine screen bordered by bright yellow daffodils and pink tulips, an Easter extravaganza of color. And there, midscreen, the photographer had grabbed a shot of seven little girls in a country church setting of flowers and ivy, each one wearing a sweet, pretty dress, suited for Easter.

That's what Rachel had risked getting into trouble for. A dress. A pretty dress like all the other little girls wore with nonchalance. A dress with ruffles and trim, or maybe a pretty bow.

He sank into the desk chair and wanted to cry, but big boys didn't cry. Did they?

Not since those first weeks after burying his beautiful wife. Cam dropped his head into his hands. Was he that bad a father? That out of tune?

Obviously so.

Could he fix it? Make amends to his girls? And to Meredith? He groaned at that, remembering the look on her face.

He'd hurt her. And he'd hurt his girls, always so sure that he knew what was best, what Kristy would have done. Sitting there with the computer screen lighting the room in pastel wonder, he realized two things: first, that Kristy loved sports but had been smart enough to realize that not every girl was born to wear cleats 24/7, and that was a lesson he should have adopted and embraced more fully.

And second, that somehow, some way, he needed to find peace with her death. Guilt had frayed a hole in his weary heart and soul, and that was his fault. Sure, he figured God was probably disgusted with him, and why wouldn't He be?

But he'd been a churchgoer before. And he had a nicely made, very dusty Bible, a wedding gift from his late grandmother. She'd written their names on the inside cover under the inscription *The Calhoun Family Bible.*

And then he'd gone and dismissed God. Ignored church, shelving the most important aspect of his girls' lives because he was embarrassed. Guilt-laden. Remorseful.

And a jerk, besides.

He brought his gaze up to the screen and made the decision he should have made long before. They would celebrate Easter as a family this year. Together. At church. And then a lovely Easter breakfast with his mother. And then the girls could hunt for eggs, just like he used to.

Meredith's image swam through his brain, and he knew he'd be doing his own version of step-toeing to fix the damage he'd done, but with God's help, he could do it. Would do it.

He shut down the computer and went to bed, his heart a mix of heavy and light, half wishing the night would hurry so he could fix the things he'd messed up, and half hoping it would take its time. Facing Meredith after his little tirade tonight? Not exactly an easy task. But…

God, I know I'm a jerk. I get that. But I want to be better. Do better. And I don't know what I was thinking all these years, not letting my girls be, well…girls. I don't know how good You are at all this girl stuff, but I need Your help. With that, and everything. Help me to relax. Bless my mom and help her to heal. Bless my girls and help them to forgive their old man for being such a stick in the mud. And while You're at it, don't let Meredith hate me. Please.

He felt better, and that was kind of strange, because he rarely felt good when he finally dropped into bed at night, and today of all days he should be hating himself.

But he didn't, and that felt nice. Real nice.

Chapter Fourteen

Meredith hit the ground running early on Saturday and didn't pause for breath. By the time Heather closed down shop at 3:00 p.m., they were tired, yet totally psyched by how many appointments they'd booked into the spa the past twenty-four hours.

Heather had put a large sign on the entrance door of the salon and one on the street side, informing people of their merger.

So far, so good. And that delighted them both.

"On Monday I'm going to approach the local papers about advertising and see if we can spawn a human-interest story about opening a new business." Meredith swept the bulk of her last trim into a dustpan, then pulled out the vacuum.

"Awesome." Heather started another load of towels in the washing machine. As it filled, she grabbed a duster. "You going to the spa now? Ready for another face-off with Cam?"

Anger and regret fought for space in Meredith's chest. "No. Mom is doing baskets for the Salvation Army Easter drive and I'm going to help her with them. Wanna come?"

"I'd love it." Heather nodded toward the Easter basket full of sweets she'd kept out for customers. "And we can add that right in because I don't want it sitting around here. I've taken off three pounds just by avoiding too much sugar and dancing with you."

"That rocks."

Heather's smile said she agreed. "If I can keep doing this, in eight more weeks it will be fifteen pounds. I could actually fit into my clothes again."

"And we'll do a little shopping," Meredith promised. "Budget-friendly, of course."

"Only way I roll around here." Heather laughed. She gathered up the morning paper and handed it to Meredith. "Can you put out the recycling bin while I start the dishwasher?"

"Of course." Meredith grabbed a sack of soda cans and water bottles. "Back in a minute." She stowed the cans in the deposit return bin, the bottles in the recycling tote, then glanced at the "Political Points of Interest" column bite on the upper left edge of the daily paper before dropping it.

Bellwater Declares Gubernatorial Run in FL.

Meredith's heart sank beyond toe level as realization struck.

Chas's wife was running for governor. That meant the incumbent would do anything to hold his seat. And "anything" meant having people dig into Sylvia Bellwater's life, delving for information to make her or her family look bad. Politics could be an ugly business behind a suit-and-tie facade. And Meredith wanted nothing to do with it, but she knew...

The gig was up because nothing escaped today's political scrutiny.

"So, girls." Cam set down the Saturday morning paper with more rustle than needed, drawing the girls' attention.

Sophie lifted calm eyes to his, a forced calm. Was her resignation due to circumstances beyond her control? If so, she'd inherited that quality from him. Time for a little more spontaneity, then.

Past time, actually.

Rachel struggled into her sneakers and he mentally added a new pair to the day's shopping list. "Are we going to Meredith's?" she asked, lips pursed, looking down, the tight shoes giving her a hard time.

He stood up, rinsed his cereal bowl and grabbed his jacket. Yesterday's cold front wasn't in any big hurry to leave, but at least the rain had tapered off. "Shopping first."

"We need groceries." Sophie acknowledged the common sense of that as she brought her bowl over. "Fridge is empty."

"I know." Cam headed to the door. "We'll get food after we shop for dresses."

"Dresses?" Sophie paused in the middle of sliding her jacket on, then turned.

"Daddy? Really?" Rachel raced across the tiles, one shoe still untied, and he caught her in his arms, reality gut-punching him. They were growing up so fast. Seven and nine. Was he too late? Had he dug in his heels too long, too deep?

"Oh, Daddy, I love you!" Rachel's grip around his neck felt good. So good. And he realized that his entrenchment had kept some of this affection at bay, just like it had with his mother. Feeling the warmth of Rachel's hug and kiss, he knelt on one knee and pulled Sophie into the embrace.

"Group hug."

They bundled like that for long seconds, entwined, him and his girls, his precious gifts from God. A tiny *mew* from the door broke them apart.

"Sally."

"Dad, look! It's Sally the kitten!"

The tiny calico had found her way to the back door, looking for love and affection and a nip of food, most likely. Cam filled a bowl with water while Sophie scooped cat food. The little kitten shivered on the porch, the cold, dank air unrelenting.

"She's cold, Daddy."

He couldn't deny it.

"And hungry," added Rachel. "Look at her eat. I wonder where she got off to?"

Sophie shook her head. "Doesn't matter. What matters is that she found her way home."

Out of the mouths of babes. Cam slung an arm around each girl, went back inside and made a warm nest of old towels in a corner of the downstairs bathroom. "Bring her in here."

"Really?"

"For real?" Rachel echoed.

He nodded. "We'll get some litter at the store, but for now we'll just tuck her in here with her food and water."

"She might make a mess, Dad." Sophie raised quiet eyes to his. "She's just a baby."

"Then we'll clean it up. Doesn't take cats long to figure out a litter box, and once she does, we can let her run around the house."

"An inside cat? Just like the Grishams?"

He was a meathead, plain and simple. "Yes. It's good to have a cat around. Keeps the mice away. And with Dora in the barn we should be all set."

"All set!" Rachel beamed at him in total agreement.

Sophie slipped her hand into his. "Thank you."

He squeezed her fingers and wondered how he could make up for the time he'd lost, then remembered the Serenity Prayer on the plaque in his bedroom. The plaque was a favorite from his childhood.

Right now he understood why the timeless words meant so much. He'd change what he could and be smart enough to know his limitations. That alone was a huge step forward. "Clock's ticking. Let's go."

They rushed ahead of him, dove into their seats and were buckled before he settled behind the wheel. No squabbling, no whining, no bickering. He sent a little prayer skyward that the stores would still have pretty dresses available at afford-

able prices. He'd phone Grandma Mary's and have them pack
an assortment of treats for tomorrow. That way he could run
in, pay the tab and pick up the bag without the girls seeing
the contents. And if he grabbed some of those marshmallow
chick things and a sack of jelly beans at the market? Perfect.

He grinned, shoved the car into Drive and aimed for town,
feeling less encumbered than he had in a long, long time.

"Dana Brennan, you brought helpers I see." The Salvation Army volunteer coordinator swung the door wide to
accommodate them. "And look at those baskets! So nice,
Dana. Thank you."

Dana waved off the thanks as she set her baskets on the row
of tables. "Glad to help. There are twenty more to bring in."

"Do tell!" The older woman followed them to the car.
When she spotted the back of the SUV, she put her hands
to her heart. "This is plenty for all the families on my list,
Dana. I thought we'd be short a few for a couple of reasons,
but you've gone and fixed the problem without even knowing there was one."

Meredith's mother hedged. "I might have had a heads-up
that one of your volunteers had a rough week."

"And it hasn't gotten better."

Dana frowned. "I'm sorry to hear that, but we were happy
to help out. That way she can concentrate on her health."

The coordinator laid a hand on Dana's shoulder. "You are
a gracious soul."

Dana shrugged that off in typical Dana style. "No big deal.
And the girls and I had fun. So, girls, let's move these inside
so they can get them distributed tonight, and then I say we
head over to the Beef Haus for some food. My treat."

"I'm in." Heather grabbed two wrapped baskets of treats
and headed back toward the door.

"Me, too." Meredith lifted her baskets, then turned back.

"What about Rory? She's done with the dance clinic in ten minutes."

"We'll pick her up."

They carted the two dozen baskets into the holding room, wished the volunteers a happy Easter, piled back into the car and turned left toward the dance studio. Halfway there, Meredith probed. "So. You did extra baskets because?"

"One of the people who'd signed up ran into some problems this week. I figured her Easter baskets might not be a big priority."

"But if they promised—"

"Sometimes life makes you forget a promise or two."

"I expect it's Mrs. Calhoun we're talking about, right?" Heather directed a questioning gaze toward Dana.

Dana looked like she didn't want to go there, but Meredith twisted in her seat. "Cam's mother?"

Heather nodded. "Alma Burlingame said she was pleased when Evelyn volunteered to donate a couple of baskets because she hadn't done any community involvement work in years."

Meredith had assumed that Evelyn was as hands-on as she used to be after their face-off at the egg hunt the week before. Obviously not.

"But when she got diagnosed with cancer earlier this week, it shook her," Heather added.

"Cancer scares people." Dana made the turn into the Donahue School of Dance stone lot and put the car into park. "But I don't feel right talking about things she might have wanted private."

"You're right." Heather made a face at herself. "I shouldn't have said anything, because Alma wasn't supposed to say anything."

"And yet she did." Dana met Heather's gaze in the mirror. "And while I love our town, that's been an ongoing problem for our family. For yours. For most, I expect."

"I'll nix the info wagon in the new spa," Heather promised. "We don't want clients into everyone's business. Was that a big problem in Maryland, Mere?"

She turned toward Meredith, but Meredith was still trying to digest that Evelyn Calhoun had cancer. No wonder Cam had been distraught. Anxious. Over the edge.

Acting like a jerk was still unacceptable, but at least now she got it. She couldn't imagine how she'd feel if Dana got sick like that. "What?"

"I was wondering if gossip was a big problem at the spa in Maryland? Or was it too big for that to be an issue?"

"Gossip is problematic everywhere." Meredith met their gazes, and went on, "And truth is, some of it was about me. If you guys have time, I'd like to tell you about it later. After we drop Rory off at home."

"Of course." Heather reached forward and pressed her cheek against Meredith's. "I love it when you admit to something less than perfection. It makes my day."

Meredith knew she was kidding and loved her for it.

Her mother laid a soft, cool hand atop hers. "I've been waiting."

Calmly and quietly, Dana had been doing just that. Meredith met her gaze of loving acceptance. "I know."

Rory hustled out the door, a jacket flung over her head. She grinned when she spotted the warm car and looked even happier at the promise of food.

Despite the lack of a father, and her mother's thin income, the girl was a sweetheart. Heather had worked to raise a wonderful kid on her own, and Meredith knew that was no simple task.

But Heather had done it, and Meredith had to make sure she wasn't about to jerk the rug out from beneath her friend's feet. She'd explain her past and let Heather decide if moving forward with the spa was in her best interests. She couldn't risk her friend's reputation and livelihood. But more than ever, Meredith hoped and prayed she'd stay because working together strengthened both of them. She only hoped Heather saw it the same way.

Meredith's phone buzzed as they dropped Rory off an hour later. She pulled it out, saw Cam's number, weighed her choices, then answered, knowing her mother and Heather would hear. "Hey. What's up?"

He didn't bother with a preamble. "I owe you an apology."

Darn straight. She hauled in a breath. "No time like the present."

"In person."

Um, no. "No can do. I'm with Mom and Heather right now and we just finished up the Salvation Army project."

"No!"

No? She paused, taken aback, then approached the exclamation with caution. "Um, yes. We really did."

"No, that's not what I mean," he went on, his words back-pedaling, his tone urgent. "I was supposed to help my mother get stuff for two baskets to donate. How did I forget that?"

The same way his mother had, Meredith figured. Something about the big C put people off their game. "No problem. Mom got enough to cover yours."

"You're kidding."

"Nope." She weighed the wisdom of what to say, and added, "She heard about your mother's illness and thought a little extra help was in order. In this one instance, gossip worked for good. And Mom's a wonder."

"Like her daughter," Cam agreed. "So, listen, about that apology."

"Unnecessary. Chalk it up to a bad day and move on. And I want you to know I'm sorry about your mother's diagnosis. It's a scary thing to go through and a tough battle to fight."

Several seconds passed before his sigh. "You're trying to

brush me off because I was a jerk. I get it. But I can make this right, Mere."

He couldn't, because her house of cards was about to fall at her feet, the very thing that pushed her from town years ago. Would she have the courage to stay? Could she? Better yet, should she?

Her mother parked the car in the drive and opened the door. Meredith used the background noise as an excuse to break the call. "Cam, we're home and I've got some stuff to do with Mom and Heather. Have a nice Easter with the girls."

She didn't wait for him to answer back, didn't hold her breath hoping he'd insist on seeing her, didn't pray he'd make amends and lead her to the happily ever after she wished was in her future. Because leading him on would only make things worse when he found out what she'd done. And Sylvia's run for office said that would likely be soon.

She disconnected the call, followed her mother and Heather into the house, sank into the overstuffed plaid sofa, tucked her feet up under her and said, "I had an affair with a senator's husband."

Chapter Fifteen

Heather's eyes went wide.

Dana's didn't. She sat next to Meredith and took her hand. "Did you know he was married?"

"No." Meredith thinned her lips and shook her head. "But that doesn't excuse it, Mom. He had a key to my apartment and a standing invitation. Bad is bad in this case."

"Explain." Heather hunched forward. "You had a relationship with this guy, but he was married. He duped you?"

"Yes." She saw their looks of indignation and swept them a "get real" look. "So, yes, he lied and used a false name, but I was the one who made it okay to have a long-term intimate relationship with a man I wasn't married to. I thought I was so cool, so now. Until it all came crashing down eighteen months ago."

"So you've been out of this relationship a long time." Dana squeezed her hand. Her face showed concern, not condemnation, even though she had to be horribly disappointed in Meredith's behavior. Behavior that reflected her cheating father's prototype. "Why did you wait to come back? To leave?"

Ah. The timeline. Meredith raised her shoulders and pinched her lips together. "A little lesson in blackmail."

"You blackmailed someone?" Her mother's carefully sculpted brows arched higher. "You didn't really. Did you?"

"No, of course not." Meredith tugged a throw pillow against her chest and scowled. "Someone blackmailed *me*. But since I wasn't exactly an innocent victim, there wasn't much I could do."

"I'm lost."

"Me, too," Heather admitted. She scootched across the rug until they formed a nice, tight circle. Three women, chatting it up. Working it out. "Explain. And start at the beginning, please. I was never good at Venn diagram stuff. Give it to me nice and slow, piece by piece."

So Meredith did, explaining how she'd met Chas, fallen in love, and developed a relationship with him that had come to a screeching halt when she discovered he was really the senator's husband and a father of three beautiful, impressionable kids. "I was blindsided, but it was my own fault for being so stupid. Thinking I was so cool. So together. It went beyond naïveté to outright stupidity. And totally my bad."

Dana shrugged. "I can't disagree. We should bear culpability for our actions, Mere. You know that. But our actions are also generated by those around us. He lied to you. Made you promises he couldn't keep. Changed his identity and then fed on your belief in him. The guy's a pig, plain and simple, and he should be called out on his behavior."

"If I'd done that, his kids would suffer." Meredith met her mother's gaze and let the past speak for her. "You and I know what that's like. I couldn't do it. But then the hotel owner's daughter decided she wanted to run the spa last fall. She threatened to go public with my indiscretions if I didn't leave my job. Evensong Resort is one of those old-guard establishments. They protect their clients at all costs. A whisper of scandal would have sent me packing anyway. I thought if I left of my own accord, I could put it all behind me. Jude Anne would get the job, and life would go on. And I'd be back home, with you." She turned her gaze to Dana and returned her mother's gentle finger pressure. "But then I saw today's paper."

Heather released a tight hiss of breath. "In the garage."

She nodded Heather's way. "Yes. A little headline that announced how Sylvia Bellwater has thrown her hat into the Florida governor's race."

"Which means the current governor will dig deep to uncover anything he can." Dana's face showed chagrin and understanding. "So it will all come out anyway."

"Which infuriates me totally." Tears she hadn't allowed welled in Meredith's eyes. "I'd like to punch somebody. Kick things. Stomp around like a little kid and throw stuff."

"You could still have at it." Her mother waved a hand around the pretty, cozy, comfy living room. "Everything here is replaceable. Except you."

"I can't wreck stuff." Meredith sighed, swiped a hand to her cheeks, accepted the wad of tissues Heather held out, and blew her nose. "It's not in me. But it's frustrating to realize it's out of my control. There's nothing I can do."

"Sure there is." Dana sent her a practical look. "We ride the wave. Okay, you had a relationship with this guy. It's over. Done. Been over for a long time once you found out you were lied to. So if people ask, that's all we need to say." She leaned forward. "Honey, come on. Do you think you're the first woman to get duped this way?"

"Of course not, but—"

"There are no buts." Dana tipped her chin up. "If you'd gone back for more, then I'd feel differently, but this is me you're talking to. I had my share of ups and downs with your father's excursions outside our marriage. I get it."

Tears welled again, because Meredith had witnessed her mother's embarrassment. Her chagrin. Her anxiety over her husband's illicit and immoral choices. "See that's just it. I hated what Dad did, I will never understand how he made those choices over us, and I turned out just like him."

Dana's mouth dropped open. Her eyes narrowed. She leaned close, very close, and spoke in soft, stern words that left no room for doubt. "*You. Are. Nothing. Like. Your. Father.* Not in that regard, anyway. If anything your behavior is like mine. You trusted too easily and got hurt. We have that in common. But honey—" She reached forward and hugged Meredith, a warm, embracing hug that made Meredith feel like a little girl again. A beloved child in her mother's arms. "You got out when you saw the writing on the wall. You're not the first young woman to be fooled, you won't be the last, but you recognize the choice and the sin, and you've worked to make amends. Now you have to forgive yourself and move on."

Meredith caught Heather's eye over her mother's shoulder, and knew the moment Heather understood the crux of the problem.

"She doesn't think she's good enough for Cam Calhoun."

Dana sat back.

Meredith scowled at Heather as she swiped the clutch of tissues against her face again. "I'm not good enough. He's got two gorgeous little girls. They don't need to have this kind of thing hanging over them if things were to progress with Cam."

"If?" Heather's eye roll said there was no *if* involved. "Name me three women involved with political scandal in the last year."

"Huh?"

"Do it." Heather sat back, all know-it-all cute and raised three fingers. "Name me three women involved with married politicians or their spouses in the past year."

"I can't."

"Exactly." Heather nodded, pleased. "Neither can I. The point is, the famous person gets remembered because he broke a vow to the people and his family. The other woman? Not so much."

"Heather's making perfect sense," Dana declared. "Yes, there will be a storm when this breaks, but storms pass. Your life will go on here with your family and friends surrounding you, while Charles and Sylvia need to pick up the personal and political pieces of their lives." She hugged Meredith and her warm, common sense, her quiet inner strength, her Mary heart in a Martha soul made Meredith feel safe. Whole. Accepted.

Yes, it would be hard when the news broke. She knew that.

But it wouldn't be impossible, and that was a big step up. "Do we have any chocolate left?"

"Absolutely." Dana rose, went into the dining room and returned with a white box. "I got these for us. Two pounds of Grandma Mary's finest with a few extra caramel pralines thrown in."

"My fave."

"And mine." Heather reached, hesitated, then took one. "One of these tonight and I'll stay away from all things chocolate tomorrow." She raised the chocolate in salute. "A toast. To family and friends and may we always appreciate good fathers because they've been a scarcity in our lives."

"I agree. Which means we need to be especially careful picking a mate. And I don't know about you, my dear—" Dana took a bite of her chocolate and smiled as the taste blossomed in her mouth "—but I think Cam Calhoun is just about the cutest thing ever with his glasses on. How adorable would he be if he took them off?"

Heather laughed out loud.

Meredith couldn't deny she'd wondered the same thing far too often. Maybe her mother was right. She might be letting the past have too much power over the present. But right now it was a wait-and-see game because protecting those little girls came first and foremost. No matter what.

* * *

There should be a commandment against a woman looking that good in church, Cam decided on Easter morning. He paused on the steps of Good Shepherd, shook the older reverend's hand, but his attention was drawn across the Park Round to the White Church at the Bend where a drop-dead gorgeous Meredith was shaking hands for too long with a thirtysomething guy.

He needed to nix that pronto, so he assembled his top two weapons. "Sophie. Rachel. I see Meredith."

"You do?"

"Where?

He jerked his head left, nodded and winked at Reverend Hannity's knowing grin, then ushered the girls down the steps. "Over there. The White Church. Shall we say—"

He didn't need to finish the sentence. Both girls raced across the town center, their pretty dresses puffing in the cool breeze, the ground still damp from yesterday's rain.

They didn't care. They trained their sights on Meredith and raced up the walk, vying for her attention, which in turn drew her attention away from the guy.

Cam put a mental plus in his score column and approached more leisurely. "They found you, I see."

Meredith smiled from the midst of a three-person hug. "So it would seem."

"Daddy, you told us she was over here." Rachel's voice scolded. "You saw her first."

Meredith's grin increased. Her eyes had a "gotcha" look that only made her prettier. More appealing. And he hadn't thought that possible, but he'd always loved her humor, that hint of snark. When it wasn't directed his way, of course.

The guy laughed, clapped a hand to Meredith's shoulder, and nodded Cam's way. "Effective ploy."

"Thank you." Cam reached out a hand. "Cam Calhoun. I'm doing the work on Meredith's spa."

"Si MacDaniel." He gripped Cam's hand and jerked his head toward the small church. "I get to work on her soul."

The new pastor. Cam wanted to gulp, but didn't. How could he compete with a man of the cloth, a man of God? He took a step back, but Dana interrupted from the side. "Cam, good morning. Happy Easter. Isn't it a glorious day?"

Her gaze embraced the two girls, each one tucked beneath one of Meredith's arm, safe and sound. Protected. Loved. Cherished. Cam met her look. "It is. And don't the girls look lovely?"

"Daddy took us shopping yesterday!" Rachel exclaimed as she tipped her gaze up. "We bought these pretty Easter dresses and my fancy shoes for church."

The look Meredith settled on him made him feel like the biggest man in town, and since he'd felt like a loser a few days before, the change was remarkable. "You look wonderful, girls. Tights, too?"

Sophie nodded and leaned against Meredith's torso, her head just shy of Meredith's chest. The image evoked mother love, trust, a joined empathy.

Cam's heart jogged faster, then readopted a nice, steady rhythm, the kind of beat that grasps God's plan and hangs on tight. "We had fun, didn't we?"

Sophie's soft smile of appreciation charged his heart a little more. "Yes. Thank you, Daddy. Oops, there's Grandma." She pointed across the park. "I think she's looking for us."

"Well, then…"

Cam waved his mother over with an easy hand, then swung back. "We're doing the Easter brunch buffet up at The Edge. We'd love for you to join us. Both of you," he added, shifting his gaze to Dana.

"I'd love to, but I can't." Dana cradled Sophie's soft cheek for just a moment, long enough to show she enjoyed the child's company. "I've got the others coming over for dinner so I have to get a few things done."

"I should help." Meredith locked gazes with her mother in a silent tug of war as Cam's mother drew near. Cam understood the inference, but he wanted Meredith to join them of her own accord. Not because he guilted her into it.

"Evelyn." Ever-gracious, Dana stretched out her hand to his mother, and to Cam's surprise, his mother accepted the gesture with unusual grace.

"Dana, hello." Back straight, she surveyed the scene, the girls snuggled into Meredith's side, the image pretty enough for an Easter card. She didn't smile, but she didn't glower either, and Cam was grateful for small steps forward. "Meredith."

"Happy Easter, Mrs. Calhoun."

The older woman considered her salute before looking at the girls. "You were very good in church. Both of you."

Sophie's soft voice interrupted everyone's shared surprise. "Thank you, Grandma."

"I was just checking to see if Meredith could join us for the buffet." Cam directed the words to his mother, but kept his gaze intent on Meredith. "If she can't drum up an excuse in the meantime."

"I'd be honored."

Cam smiled his pleasure at the positive answer and tapped his watch. "We've got midday seating so we should head over there. I've heard this buffet is amazing."

"Expensive."

Evelyn bit the word out, and Meredith expected Cam's customary chagrin.

Didn't happen.

Instead, he slung an arm around his mother's shoulders and kissed her temple, sweet as could be. "Doesn't matter since I'm paying. I got this nice-paying extra job, you know." He winked at Meredith, nodded to Dana and Si MacDaniel, then turned his mother toward the opposite side of the town circle. "She's paying me well, you need to rest and I'm a lousy cook." He turned, teasing, to look at Meredith. "How 'bout you, Miss Brennan? Have you learned to cook?"

"I can find my way around a kitchen."

"Great."

"As long as it has a microwave," she finished.

Cam grinned. "The girls and I love takeout."

Meredith half expected a cutting comment from Evelyn along the lines of women knowing their place, women taking up outside the home, women getting all gussied up, but, no. Evelyn just walked alongside her son, as if fighting the urge to be ill-natured and winning.

Chalk one up for Easter, Meredith decided, then realized her assumption was mean. Determined to do better, she took the backseat with the girls. Cam caught her eye in the rearview mirror as he turned the car around. "So, that new young preacher?"

"Simon?"

"Yes."

"He's a doll."

Evelyn harrumphed. Obviously calling pastors "dolls" didn't make the cut.

"How long's he been here?"

Meredith considered the question. "Over a year. Maybe two. Matt and Jeff told me about him, and Mom and I like to church-hop, so we got to meet him along the way."

"Married?"

She held his gaze while the car was paused at the stoplight heading out of the village. "Single."

"Ah."

Meredith could have let him suffer a while. He had been a first-class jerk the other night, but now she knew the underlying reasons and he *had* called to apologize. She angled her head and flirted right then and there, with his mother and girls close by. "He lost by default, Cam."

Cam's smile said he got her drift. "How's that?"

"No glasses."

He laughed out loud.

His mother sighed.

Rachel held out a round of yarn. "Can you do cat's cradle, Meredith?"

"Reigning town expert, my dear."

Rachel frowned.

Sophie leaned closer, her often somber eyes warm and appealing. Happy and calm. Seeing that expression on the quiet girl's face made Meredith's day. "That means she's good, Rachel. But out of practice, I bet."

Meredith refused to concede that. "Her first. You, next. If there's time."

"Plenty of that, I'd say." Cam sought her gaze in the rearview mirror. "Traffic's bottlenecked."

Meredith deftly looped the yarn from Rachel's splayed hands. "Perfect."

· And sitting there on a cool Easter morning, with Cam and the girls and one slightly grumpy cancer-fighting elderly woman, Meredith felt like things couldn't possibly get better.

"It's awful busy." Evelyn's grumpy tone admonished Cam as he hunted for a parking space. "We'll probably be waiting a long time for a table."

"Well, it *is* Easter." Cam's voice stayed matter-of-fact. Meredith envied him the lack of reaction, when she was more inclined to scold right back. "And we've got reservations, Mom."

"Oh, that's right."

Meredith's fingers paused over the intricate yarn web Sophie proffered. Once again, Evelyn's reaction surprised her.

In a nice way.

And when they climbed out of the car and Sophie grabbed her right hand while Rachel commandeered the left, Evelyn took note and almost smiled.

Progress.

Cam put an arm around his mother's shoulders. "Mom, what do you think about putting a patch of those daffodils along your back walk? Wouldn't that be pretty in the spring?"

"Don't need more work, Cameron."

"If they're mulched properly, it won't be extra work. But it sure would brighten things up, wouldn't it?" He sent his mother a look that loosened Meredith's heart further. "I'll plant them for you this fall and you can enjoy them next spring."

Evelyn's expression confessed worry that there might not be a next spring, but she stood a little straighter and acquiesced. "Pretty enough, I guess."

"Maybe a few lilac bushes, too," Cam continued. "Then you'd have flowers in April and May."

"Lilacs were always my favorite," his mother revealed as they entered the hillside restaurant. Inside, white twinkle lights brightened vine-wrapped pillars, and tucks of flowers proclaimed warmth despite the cool, damp weather. Evelyn looked up as Cam held her seat out for her. "I'd like that, Cameron. Thank you."

He planted a kiss on her hair. The simple gesture said so much about the man. His patience, his kindness, his generous spirit.

But he'd grumped at her more than once recently, and Meredith wasn't a big fan of being reproached. Or contradicted. Or reprimanded. Not by him or his mother.

"Coffee?"

"Yes. Please." Meredith smiled at the waitress, grateful for the interruption. She didn't want to spoil a beautiful day by waxing negative. She'd take her mother's advice and move forward, one day at a time.

"Me, too." Cam tipped his gaze down. "Girls?"

"May I have orange juice, please?" Sophie asked.

"Me, too?" Rachel echoed.

"And you, ma'am?" The waitress shifted her attention to Cam's mother.

"You got decaf?"

The girl didn't miss a beat. "We do, yes."

Evelyn huffed a sigh. "I'll drink that, then."

Cam frowned. "Why?"

The waitress hesitated.

The girls looked up, wondering.

"They say it's better for you." Evelyn muttered the words through tight teeth. "Claire Dennehy read it somewhere."

"She's wrong." Cam turned toward the young woman. "Make hers regular coffee, too, please. And do you have flavored creamers?"

The waitress nodded. "Yes."

"Wonderful. And thank you for working on Easter."

"You're welcome." She smiled. "We split shifts so everyone gets family time, and I did the sunrise service with my folks hours ago. And we close at three today, so it's just the brunch crowd."

"Smart." Meredith nodded at the crowded room. "And there's strudel on that buffet, right?"

The girl laughed. "Every kind known to man, including the new pineapple cheese variety. I don't think we could open the doors in the morning without Susan Langley's strudel."

She moved to gather their drinks, while Cam intercepted Meredith's look of appraisal. "You're thinking something."

"I do that now and again." She handed a pack of crayons over to Rachel and nodded at the table. "You can decorate the tablecloth for Easter if you like."

"But it's cloth," Sophie protested.

"Vinyl, actually. And the crayons wash out. That's why they have them here."

"Coloring on other people's things?" Evelyn's tone edged up. "Don't seem right to me."

The waitress returned with their drinks, saw the crayons

and gave the girls a quick nod of permission. "Have at it, girls. It's fun to decorate while you wait for your food. Alyssa found these cloths online and we've been using them ever since. The kids love them." She directed the last line toward Cam and his mother.

Evelyn eyed her, then fingered the smooth vinyl blend. "It really washes out? They don't get ruined?"

"No, ma'am."

"Amazing."

"It is, isn't it?"

The girls dove into the box, but sat back, mouths open, when Evelyn joined in. As she sketched a small garden between her and Rachel, a spark of recognition brightened Cam's gaze. "I forgot you liked to draw."

Evelyn shrugged.

"Mom, you're good."

"Very good." Meredith leaned closer. "That's an amazing talent, Mrs. Calhoun."

"Bah." She sat back, withdrew a light green and shaded in tiny arcs of leaves, then began filling the foreground with pastel blooms.

"Do you draw at home?" Meredith asked.

Evelyn shook her head. "No."

"Why not?"

"What for?" When Meredith looked perplexed, Evelyn frowned. "If it don't serve a purpose, why do it?"

"For your enjoyment? Relaxation? Personal therapy?"

Evelyn waved that off. "When folks worry too much about themselves, they get stuck."

Meredith didn't mention that Evelyn had spent a lot of time worrying about others' business and not minding her own. A different kind of stuck. "Balance, then."

Evelyn's fingers hesitated. Listening? Yes. And that was good.

Their table was called. Meredith and the girls hung back.

allowing Cam to escort Evelyn to the buffet first. Meredith took a moment to study Evelyn's artistic effect. Her miniature garden showed intrinsic technique with a flourish of whimsy.

The whimsy came as a total surprise.

Which meant Evelyn might be more than she'd seemed years ago. But Meredith and her family had suffered from Evelyn's sharp tongue, her carved-in-stone opinions. Latitude hadn't existed in Evelyn's world, but maybe it had seemed worse because of Meredith's age. And the fact that Evelyn didn't think her good enough for Cam.

A fact Meredith had proven.

Don't go there. Her mother's advice buffered her. *Forgive yourself and move on.*

With their hands clasped firmly in hers, Meredith guided the two girls to the beginning of the buffet line, determined to do just that.

Chapter Sixteen

Cam missed the days when Easter was followed by a week off. He hit the ground running on Monday morning and worked nonstop all week long without a glimpse of Meredith. If she meant to tweak his interest by playing hard to get, he graded the ploy an A-plus.

His mother had scheduled an appointment with the laryngeal cancer surgeon in Rochester for Friday. Cam arranged for a day off, and debated asking Meredith to take the girls after school. The weekend would begin spring break, a welcome reprieve, but with the busyness of a holiday/holy day weekend behind them, the girls were tired, fractious and downright ornery by seven o'clock at night.

Not exactly courting grounds, he supposed.

By Thursday he realized his stupidity and the foolishness of leaving life to chance. He called Meredith's cell phone and tried to fight a grin when she answered.

Impossible.

He was driving back to the high school from the newly repaired house site, so he had to talk quickly. "I need your help, Mere."

"With?"

"My mom has an appointment with a cancer specialist

tomorrow. It's in Rochester, so I need to take the day off to get her up there. Would you take the girls after school? I don't know how long we'll be, Kristy's parents don't come into town until Sunday, and the Grishams are leaving town for spring break."

Meredith didn't hesitate, which said nice things about her after the way he went off on her the last time she had the girls. "Glad to. Shall I pick them up at school?"

"That would be great."

"What time?"

The anxiety of a crazy four days quieted with her voice, her words, her melodic tone spiking old memories and new thoughts. "Three-fifteen."

"Can do. And, um…" She waffled, then continued, "No restrictions, right? We get to do whatever girl things we choose."

"Within the boundaries of the law, yes."

She laughed. "Better, Cam. Much better."

He *felt* better, talking with her. Laughing with her. He wasn't stupid. He'd seen how she and his mother choreographed a careful dance with one another. But his mother's attitude showed hints of improvement. Was that because his behavior had changed, or because her diagnosis had made her rethink things?

Either way, he was grateful for the upswing. "Then can we do dinner together on Sunday? Kristy's parents are taking the girls to Florida for the week. It's a yearly tradition, and I love that they want to be part of the girls' lives, but I miss them like crazy that first night."

"I bet you do." Meredith paused. "Yes. I'll have dinner with you, Cam. I'd like that."

"Me, too."

By Sunday evening, it felt like she'd been waiting forever. Knowing that emotional storm waters were gathering ahead of their date, Meredith couldn't let herself relax in the moment. Not too much, anyway. But oh, how she wanted to.

"You look—" Cam took a long, languorous moment to study her before lifting both shoulders in a shrug "—stunning. It's the best I've got."

The best he had was more than good enough. "Couldn't ask for more. Are we going to The Edge?"

He shook his head, took her hand and led her to his car. "Not tonight."

"Then?"

He put one workman's finger to her lips. "You'll see. You don't mind a little drive, do you?"

Daylight savings time meant light tarried longer. The sun hung above them and slightly west, blazing its way to the horizon, peach-streaked clouds striating the soft blue background. "Not at all."

"Good."

He didn't kiss her, but he looked like he wanted to, and that only led to her wanting it right back. He sent her a look confirming the feeling. "I'm thinking what you're thinking, but the nice thing about kissing you? Wanting to kiss you?"

She angled her head in question. "Is?"

"Knowing it doesn't seem to want to go away. Ever."

Her heart softened even as red flags sprouted.

But what had Simon preached that very morning? The third chapter of Ecclesiastes, a favorite of so many. "To everything there is a season, and a time for every purpose under the heaven…"

What if this was their season? Hers and Cam's? It felt that way, a door thrown open, a curtain drawn aside. Did she dare step through? Or should she just tell him everything straight out and let fate have its day?

Yes.

Tonight?

She squirmed in her seat.

Cam thrust a quizzical brow up as he made the turn onto I-86. "Stop worrying. This isn't a night to share war stories, Mere. Unless you want it to be."

The ticking bomb of Sylvia's gubernatorial run almost made her say yes. Get things out in the open. Confess. Baring her soul was better than crouching in shadows.

Another part wanted to relax in the moment, spend a few hours with the wonderful man at her side, and be Cam's girl, one more time. "No. Not tonight. But soon, Cam. Because I need to be up-front with you. Honest. I've been gone a long time, and things happen."

Cam knew that. He'd relived the guilt of finding his lifeless, beautiful wife time and again. So Meredith had a story to tell?

So did he.

But he was pretty sure she'd never killed anyone, so if it came to a contest, his truth would outweigh hers most likely. And that knowledge shamed him to the core.

"Well, the girls are gone until next weekend. We can schedule a heart-to-heart at your convenience."

"Things like that are rarely convenient." Her wry expression deepened the meaning. "But necessary."

"On a different note." He turned toward Route 305 and sent her sidelong glance. "Mom's surgery is set for the end of the week."

"Whoa. Fast."

"Yes, but I might need help again. The recovery with this is supposed to be really quick, but just in case Mom needs assistance, I want to be on hand. And I have to take her up there and bring her back. The girls come back late Saturday. If I need you to grab them, is that all right?"

"Cam, I'm happy to do it. Your girls are amazing. And they like me. Go figure."

"They're falling in love with you." He laid the words ou carefully, appraising her reaction.

Pure Meredith, plain and simple. "Like their father?" She turned in her seat as she said it, up-front and honest. Direct There were moments he didn't embrace that quality in her Right now it was fine. Just fine.

"Yes."

She grinned and tapped his shoulder like an old buddy would. "Sweet. We'll just see how that all works out, my friend."

"Except I wasn't kidding around." He parked the car a Moonwinks, a long-established restaurant tucked in Cuba New York, climbed out his side while she exited hers, an faced her over the roof. "One of us was being serious."

She braced her arms on the car top. "Me, too. But we jus scheduled a war-stories date and I don't think either of u should jump into the romance waters too soon. Not until we clear them up some."

Cam had muddied plenty of water in his time, but he couldn't imagine Meredith doing anything to wear this much on her heart. Her soul. But fourteen years?

He rounded the car, slipped his hands around her waist and settled a kiss to her mouth, all gentleness and warmth "Then we'll talk. But I can't imagine anything you have to say will change the way I feel, Mere. Just having you here Having you back?" He pulled back and smiled. "Brightens my days. And I'm not opposed to commitments that would change my nights, as well."

She blushed and dropped her head to his chest. "Me, either But while I'd love for that to happen, Cam…" She squared her shoulders and faced him, her expression doubtful. "I don' know that it can, in all honesty."

"Then we'll see, won't we?" He wouldn't push further to night. But soon, because whatever dragon dogged her path he needed to slay it.

* * *

She was about to kidnap Evelyn Calhoun.

Meredith stopped the car Thursday morning, scanned the old Calhoun house, and gripped the steering wheel with two hands.

Evelyn thought Meredith was picking her up for a quick cut, the same bob the old woman had worn for the twenty years that Meredith had known her.

Meredith had other ideas. And while Heather didn't have the equipment or space for a full spa day, CeeCee had volunteered her services for a therapeutic massage, and Meredith had commandeered a nail tech for a pedicure, and Meredith would do the hair.

If Evelyn didn't run screaming.

Meredith sent up a little prayer for guidance, then approached the house.

Evelyn met her at the porch. Her usual scowl had taken a holiday, but she didn't look all that pleasant, either. "Cameron could've got me."

"He could have," Meredith agreed. She put out an arm for Evelyn, and refused to take offense when her gesture was rebuffed. "But he's got this week to work on the spa renovations and I'm free today because Heather's shop isn't as busy on Thursdays, so it made sense for me to come over. Unless it makes things too difficult for you." Meredith paused and put a hand on Evelyn's arm. "Because I don't want to do that, Mrs. Calhoun."

Evelyn grimaced, but shrugged it off. "It's fine. I taught Cam to work hard for what he wanted. Seems foolish now to criticize him because he listened, don't it?"

Meredith smiled. "A little."

"Ach." Evelyn pulled open the passenger door and climbed in. "Let's get this done."

Not exactly the most gracious acquiescence in Meredith's

life, but considering the who and the what and the where
Not too bad, either.

When they pulled into the small salon lot, Evelyn spotte
the door and shrank back. "What's this?"

Meredith grinned once she came around to the passer
ger side. "It's Evelyn Calhoun day. Just like the sign on th
door says."

"It's no such thing." Evelyn clung to the car, eyeing th
banner, then Meredith. "I don't like to be embarrassed, your
lady."

"Not embarrassed. Pampered." Meredith drew her fo
ward. "Today you are going to get the full benefit of spa re
laxation techniques as developed by the best of the best i
America and Europe."

"Including hair color, cut, style, mani, pedi and massage
Heather bustled through the door, saw Evelyn's look an
laughed out loud. "Mrs. Calhoun, you've known me foreve
Trust me on this—you're about to have the time of your life

"I—"

"Don't hold for such nonsense." Meredith interrupted th
spiel and continued into the salon. "But when you're stresse
or sick, or tired out, being cared for can be good for the hea
and soul. I promise. Think of it the way you would if Ca
was sick. Or Julia and Mark."

While Meredith had a tough time envisioning a young
Evelyn as a gentle mom, her words touched something insi
the older woman. "I took good care of them."

Meredith nodded. "Which is exactly what we're going
do for you. With your permission, of course."

The moment of truth had arrived. Would Evelyn acce
this olive branch? Or would she snip and snipe and cut the
down to size? Seconds passed with the tick of the wall cloc
marking time before Evelyn thumped her two-decades-o
purse onto a side table. "That coffee smells mighty good."

Heather gave her a shoulder hug. "Coming right up. Ar

Jeannine is our nail tech today, so she's going to start you off with a spa pedicure."

"These old feet are none too pretty," Evelyn demurred, looking at her worn shoes.

"They will be." Jeannine stowed Evelyn's belongings in the front room, then led Evelyn to the pedicure chair as though royalty ascending a throne. And when Evelyn bent to remove her shoes and rolled-down knee-highs, Jeannine intervened with a gentle hand. "Allow me. You just sit back. Relax into the chair. Today it's my day to do the work."

"Okay."

Meredith and Heather exchanged looks of triumph. Yes, Cam's mother sounded dubious. But she'd given permission, enough to get the ball rolling, and who wouldn't feel better about just about everything after a spa pedicure?

No one they knew.

The ring of the salon phone interrupted the moment of victory. Meredith answered it, smiling. "Heather's Salon, Meredith speaking. How can I help you?" She frowned when no response came, then placed the hand piece back on the receiver. "Wrong number, most likely."

Her cell jangled a few minutes later, but this time an excited Sophie answered from the other end. "Meredith! Rachel and I just went on a pirate boat with Grandma and Grandpa!"

"Were you kidnapped, dear?"

Sophie laughed out loud, her joy contagious. "No, they have a real pirate ship down here and you can take rides on it, but they did kidnap some people. Just not us. I think it's because Rachel looked scared."

If anyone looked nervous, Meredith would bet on Sophie, and Rachel's background indignation attested that.

"Did not!"

"Did, too," Sophie told her in a loud aside. "And hush, it's my turn to talk, not yours. Meredith?"

"I'm here, honey. And be nice to your sister. She's littler."

"I know. Sorry. And they said they *do* throw a few people to the sharks from time to time, but not anyone on our trip. So that was good!"

"That's excellent, honey. Your dad will be so pleased to hear you were not consumed by huge carnivorous fish with giant teeth. Phew!"

"You're funny."

Meredith grinned. "You, too. Did your sister like the pirates?" Meredith envisioned Rachel on the pirate ship, appraising the setup, vying for control. Those pirates had no idea who they were dealing with.

"I'll let her tell you."

"Mere?"

Rachel's one word spiked high. "Yes, honey?"

"I'm having the best day of my life."

"Oh, that's wonderful."

Evelyn's head shifted right. Their conversation had drawn her attention. Meredith winked across the room and said, "Hey, Grandma's here with me. Tell her about it."

She didn't wait for permission, but handed Evelyn the phone. Flustered, Evelyn studied the small cell phone, and then held it to her ear. "Hello?"

Meredith cringed inside, understanding the sensitive microphone feature, and hoping Rachel's hearing would withstand the onslaught. Evelyn repeated the word, then frowned and wagged the phone. "I can't hear a thing."

"Try this." Meredith turned on the speakerphone feature. "Is that better?"

"Hi, Grandma!"

Evelyn brightened. Meredith decided to jot down the day and the hour for posterity.

"Rachel. Are you having fun?"

"So much! We got stolen by pirates and we almost had to walk the plank!"

"Well, good thing Daddy got you those swimming lessons when you were little."

"That's what I thought, too."

Meredith moved out of earshot to allow Evelyn some private time with the girls. True, they'd called to talk to her, but helping them bridge their relationship with their Grandma Calhoun seemed like a good thing. And if Evelyn's attitude continued to improve, well...she might enjoy having the girls around more often.

Evelyn held up the phone. "They had to go have lunch."

"Awesome." Meredith pocketed the phone with a smile. "They sound like they're having a great time."

"The DeRoses can afford to do things like that with them."

Meredith waved that off as inconsequential. "They can't teach them to draw. Or to put up applesauce for the winter. Or to make that sour cherry jam you used to make. I don't think I've ever tasted anything better than your sour cherry jam."

"Really?" Evelyn's face softened, as if the idea of anyone loving her jam was too great an accomplishment. "I haven't made that in years."

"Maybe this year, then. The girls would enjoy learning that kind of thing."

"And you know this because?"

Meredith sank into the chair opposite Cam's mother. "My mom and I baked with them the last time they were over. That's the nuts and bolts they miss about not having a mother, because they really don't remember Kristy that well."

Evelyn's face shadowed. "Rachel don't remember her at all."

"No."

"Well, then I'll do it, I suppose. Once we get this—" she waved a hand at her throat "—done with."

"They'll love it."

"Would you mind helping?"

Emotion welled in Meredith's chest. Her throat tightened.

Her chin wanted to quiver, but she held firm. Cam's mother was asking for her help. And today, she was *accepting* her help. Would wonders never cease? Meredith stood, smiled, and laid a hand on Evelyn's shoulder. "I'd love to. First, we'll tackle cancer…."

A little smile and a firm nod accented that idea.

"And then kitchen skills."

"You've got a deal. And now, can you help me pick a color from this tray, young lady?" Evelyn asked. She pinched her lips in question, then relaxed back into a smile. "Something that goes with old and wrinkled would be good."

Meredith laughed, helped Evelyn select a subdued country rose, then chatted with her while Jeannine finished the pedicure.

Had the cancer diagnosis changed Evelyn to this degree? Or was it the result of time? Of prayer?

Probably all three, Meredith decided, but whatever the cause, she was gratified to spend an enjoyable day with Cam's mother, an achievement she wouldn't have considered possible a few weeks back.

Meredith had made over his mother.

Cam's head reeled with that reality.

He'd walked into the house and found an updated version of Evelyn Calhoun waiting for him. Fresh coffee filled the pot, and cookies…yes, fresh-baked cookies…filled a plate on the table.

Obviously he'd entered an alternate universe through some secret portal, but he had no desire to turn back. The cookies smelled too good.

"You baked."

She nodded as if she did this kind of thing all the time, and a little nerve inside Cam tweaked his brain. She had baked when they were young. Before Dad died.

"I want to get in practice again, but it seems like some

things you don't forget." She jutted her chin toward the plate, then the oven. "I put these together just as easy as pie without lookin' up the recipe in my box, but I can't for the life of me remember where I set my glasses down. Memory's a funny thing."

"It is." Cam took two cookies, accepted the cup of coffee she poured him and tried not to choke on the surprise of his mother acting like a benevolent host. He sighed in delight when he bit into the first. "These are the best you ever made."

She preened. And with her new hair color accenting her updated cut and curl…and was that makeup she had on? He squinted and was pretty sure it was.

The smile made her look downright pretty. "Mom, you look beautiful."

She sat in the chair alongside him, made a face, but couldn't hide her pleasure at his words. "Oh, go on."

"I mean it. And you were okay with Meredith and Heather doing this?"

"Them girls are nice." She leaned forward and tapped the table with force, then frowned and checked her nails before she met his gaze. "I never held for such things, I know, but Meredith was right about it relaxing you. I felt so good when they were done. And not just the primping, but having my shoulders and back massaged. Land sakes, Cameron, I felt like a new woman."

"Well, you look wonderful. And I'm glad you had fun. And these cookies?" He raised a third into the air, and that broadened her smile. "The best ever. Can you teach the girls how to do this sometime?"

"Exactly why I'm practicing." She jumped up, withdrew a recipe box from the corner of a glass-fronted cupboard, and settled it carefully, as though the contents were fragile. "In here are all my old recipes. Meredith and I are going to teach the girls a thing or two. If it's all right," she added, looking at him for confirmation.

"It's fine."

More than fine, he wanted to shout, but he left it low-key, sure his mother would think him whacked if he jumped in the air. No, simple delight was better, he knew that, but inside?

He was dancing for joy. His mother would go into surgery tomorrow looking good, feeling good, with a mindset of faith and confidence. Coupled with the good doctor's expertise, he couldn't ask for more, but he did. Seeing his mother's peace and comfort, he sent up a prayer that God watch over her. Guide the surgeon's hands. Because he really, truly wanted his mother around for a long while, a chance for the girls to know and love this side of Evelyn Calhoun.

The side he'd pretty much forgotten.

He called Meredith as soon as he got behind the wheel.

No answer.

He scowled, wondered if he should track her down, but had no idea where she might be. Obviously busy, or she'd have answered her phone. He left a message extolling his gratitude, but wished he could thank her in person. The gradual changes in his mother, in his relationship with her, in his heart, and yes, maybe even his soul...

Wondrous summed it up.

He headed home and cleaned up. He decided not to bother with the internet because he needed to have his mother in Rochester by 9:00 a.m. and that meant an early start.

He went to bed, tired but pleased, and Cam couldn't remember the last time he'd put those two things together, but tonight he did. Thankfully.

Chapter Seventeen

"Meredith Brennan?"

The moment Meredith heard the words, she knew the jig was up but refused to react overtly.

Inside?

Her gut jellied.

"You are Meredith Brennan, aren't you?"

Meredith moved to shrug by the guy, but he pulled out a small pad. Too late, she saw a photographer snapping shots to his left. The *zip-click* of the camera said more than words ever could.

"Miss Brennan, did you have an affair with Charles Bellwater while living in Beaumont, Maryland?"

She pushed past, then felt a quick, strong arm at her flank. "Come on, Mere."

Heather. Thank You, God.

Heather steered her toward the car, helped shield her from the camera as she ducked in, then rounded the car in record time, climbed in, and set the clutch with lightning speed. "I expect this will move them."

She popped into gear.

Oh, they moved, all right. The reporter dodged right, the

photographer stepped left, and Heather barreled out of the parking lot with a Hollywood-worthy squeal of rubber.

"Morons."

Meredith wouldn't disagree, but she also understood one thing: they were doing their job. And they wouldn't stop. She frowned, realized Heather was heading north, not south, and turned. "Where are you going?"

"Megan Romesser's old apartment."

Megan had lived in the furnished apartment above her cookie store in Jamison before she got married. "Because?"

Heather sidled her a look. "Your mother just called me. They're everywhere, Mere."

Oh, God, no. Please, no. I'm not ready. I haven't told Cam. I haven't...

Too late, she realized. Obviously the press had the story, and they'd hunt her down like bloodhounds, relentless. Persistent. And they wouldn't give up until they captured their prey.

She put a hand on Heather's arm and when Heather glanced her way, Meredith jerked her head. "Turn around."

"Huh?"

"Head back."

"No."

Meredith sighed, shrugged and gave her old friend a slightly worn smile. "Yes. Come on, Heather. You know it's the right thing to do. And I promised myself I'd face things head-on for the rest of my life. Starting now."

Heather's eyes went moist, and Meredith needed to staunch her friend's rising sympathy. If Heather got emotional, Meredith would lose it, too, and she didn't want that. "You told me you know one of the columnists for the *Wellsville Daily Reporter,* right?"

Heather's face brightened, catching her drift. "Yes."

Meredith dialed her mother's number. "Let's see how she'd feel about an exclusive. Cut these guys off at the pass. Jerk the rug out from under their feet."

"Because if the story's already out there…"

"They've got nothing new to report."

"Exactly. The best defense—"

"Is a well-executed offense." Meredith finished the thought for her friend. "If someone's going to benefit from this, I'd rather it be the hometown paper than some national scandal sheet."

"I concur." Heather turned the car around and headed back toward Wellsville, but she shot Meredith a quick look of question. "You're sure?"

Knowing what was at stake? That Cam would have every reason to walk away and never look back? To shrug her off and keep her from his beautiful daughters? No, she wasn't a bit sure, but she also knew it was the right thing to do.

To everything there is a season….

This season, the truth would set her free. She'd see to it.

The surgeon shook Cam's hand, handed him a prescription for painkillers his mother could take if needed, and turned to face Evelyn. "It looks good, Mrs. Calhoun. We'll keep a close check on you initially, so you'll be taking some trips back and forth, but the surgery went well. No problems. And we'll keep our eye on things."

Evelyn nodded. "Thank you, Doctor."

"My pleasure."

Cam took her arm as they went to the car, and she raised a thoughtful hand to her throat. "It's hard to imagine that's it."

"For treatment?"

"Yes." She met his look, stopped, and hugged him. "I wouldn't have even gone looking for a solution like this if you hadn't pressured me."

"Well—"

"Thank you, son. It means a lot to me."

Him, too. Helping her, being nice, being the son he should

have been? All good. He opened the car door. "Hop in. Let's get you home and see what's cooking in Allegany County."

He rued the words the minute he stepped into the Crossroads mini-mart to gas up an hour later. His mother had dozed off thirty minutes into the trip and hadn't awakened as yet. Which was probably a good thing because Cam found himself tempted to inflict bodily harm on two men in the store, and his mother wouldn't approve.

"She sold that story, no doubt." The one man held up a copy of the *Wellsville Daily,* while the other guy scowled at the picture of Meredith flanked by her mother and Heather Madigan.

"Most likely. Women like that will do anything, and she'll probably be cutting a cushy book deal soon."

"Stinkin' tell-all." The first guy handed over a card to the clerk, signed the receipt, then gathered his things. "We got nothing here. Best thing to do is leave it alone. The story's out, she pulled the surprise factor out from under us, and I expect the town will do damage enough. Hole-in-the-wall towns like this don't like loose women hanging around."

"Some factions might." The photographer leered.

The leer did it.

The combination of their words, attitude, and the article that proclaimed Meredith as Charles Bellwater's lover pushed Cam over the edge. In the blink of an eye, calm, cool Cam Calhoun had the first guy up against a wall of canned goods. The second guy backed off, hands raised. "Since you're leaving town anyway, let me just help you to the door." Cam steered the man toward the door with quick steps.

"I don't mind offering an assist." Brett Stanton came from behind the counter and grabbed the other guy's arm. "I was making a sandwich at the lunch counter, and didn't think too highly of how these guys were describing our town's latest entrepreneur."

"Me, either."

The mouthy reporter began a tirade about lawsuits, rights' infringement and freedom of the press.

"There's a couple of sheriffs right there." Cam inclined his head toward two patrol cruisers parked side by side along the curb. "I'm sure they'd love to hear your complaints. I do believe one of them is Meredith Brennan's cousin."

"So it is." Brett followed Cam's lead and kept his voice nonchalant. "That's Zach Walker. Let's see if I can get their attention."

"No."

"Never mind."

The two loudmouths went real quiet at the thought of meeting up with the maligned woman's uniformed cousin.

"Get out." Cam stared the guy down, released his arm, and jerked a thumb to the car. "And don't come back. And if your mother forgot to teach you the Thumper rule, you might do well to look it up."

They pulled away with a spin of loose gravel.

Part of Cam felt good.

Another part had been sucker-punched. This was what Meredith had wanted to tell him. He was sure of it. The look in her eyes, the shame, the longing. The sorrow.

He'd read the emotions and put it off, and now she'd come face-to-face with the Maryland past she'd fled.

His heart twisted in realization. She'd run away from Allegany County years ago, when things got rough, unable to deal with the gossip, heat and derision. What would she do now? Run? Stay?

Run, most likely.

He turned and stuck out a hand to Brett. "Hey, thanks. I appreciate your help."

Brett shrugged it off. "Right place. Right time. And I like Meredith Brennan. I went by the spa to do a fire code inspection yesterday morning, and she's, well…" He shrugged. "A nice lady. Doesn't deserve junk like that. And there were guys like these two crawling all over town yesterday, hunting her down. I've never been a big fan of reporters. Glad to help."

The words meant more because Brett wasn't the kind of guy who mixed or mingled unless it was with the fire department. As a crew chief, he stayed involved in helping others, but from the outside looking in. Always.

"Well, your military training came in handy, Chief. Thank you."

Brett nodded, waved a quick but not unfriendly hand toward the two sheriffs and headed back inside.

Reporters crawling all over town? No wonder she hadn't answered her phone last night. And he'd gone off to bed, unaware.

Guilt prickled until he realized that unaware meant she hadn't turned to him. Hadn't come to him. And that most likely, given a choice, Meredith would run.

Again.

Chapter Eighteen

The ringing doorbell ignited Meredith's adrenaline Saturday morning. Her mother's expression said the caller wasn't Cam, but she didn't shut the door in the visitor's face, so it wasn't a reporter, either. Jude Anne Geisler's father walked into her mother's living room, spotted Meredith and gave a quick nod. "I know why you left."

Because he was about the last person on earth Meredith expected to see, her reaction time stumbled.

"And we want you back." Kevin Geisler spread his hands, his expression apologetic. "Jude Anne can't handle the rigors of a job like this. I thought she could. Hoped she could. But when I found out what happened with Chas, Charles, whatever his name is, it all made sense. And because my daughter was stressed after trying to run a business that takes a certain amount of finesse she doesn't possess, she confessed that she pushed you into leaving."

"Blackmailed her, you mean." Dana met his look of apology with one of quiet determination. "Your daughter blackmailed Meredith, costing her livelihood, her accrued time, her pension investments and threatening her good name. If we put this into evidentiary proceedings, any judge worth his salt would find reason to hold her accountable in both civil and criminal court."

"Mom." For the first time, Meredith caught a glimpse of her grandmother in her mother, and loved it, but she knew Kevin was blameless. Other than loving his spoiled daughter, the man was innocent of wrongdoing in the whole mess.

He had the grace not to fumble the ball. "I can't disagree. And the fact that Charles Bellwater is a lying, conniving, cheating scoundrel who was willing to change his identity to prey on women disgusts me." He turned back to Meredith. "Jude Anne did you wrong."

No doubt of that. "Yes."

"And so did Bellwater."

Meredith couldn't pretend innocence she didn't feel. "He lied, yes. And I had no idea he was married, and I broke things off as soon as I found out. But I entered the relationship of my own accord, and that was my own foolishness."

He accepted her words with poise. "Love does funny things to people." His steady gaze said he understood that more than most. "And everyone makes mistakes, but you shouldn't have had to pay for it with your job. Our policy of avoiding scandal put you between a rock and a hard place because of my daughter. Yes—" he turned toward Dana and dipped his chin "—I'm willing to make monetary amends for all Meredith lost, but more than that, I'd like to offer her the job back. With a five-year contract, a hefty raise, guaranteed investiture and an opt-out clause on her part only."

A guaranteed job.

A raise.

No one could fire her, and she could continue to seek the training of the best of the best with quick trips to Washington, Philly, New York and Boston.

"I—"

"I don't expect an on-the-spot answer." Kevin moved forward. "We put you in a predicament, and my family will bear that responsibility. Even if it requires the law, Mrs. Brennan."

Dana studied him a long moment before shifting her attention back to Meredith. "My daughter and I will discuss this."

"Yes." Meredith acknowledged her mother's wisdom, then turned her attention back to Kevin. "You fired Jude Anne?"

He nodded. "But then her mother swooped in, dried her tears as usual, and picked up all the pieces before carting her off to Europe."

Another example of how messy divorce can get. Despite Jude Anne being nearly thirty, her mother coddled her. And if they did have grounds for a lawsuit, getting Jude Anne back here would be nothing but work and aggravation.

Meredith was already aggravated enough, but she'd learned a lesson from her mother. Decisions made in haste come back to haunt you. "I'll consider the offer and the legalities, Kevin. But I want you to know one thing." She stepped forward and stuck out her hand. "No matter what happens, I thoroughly enjoyed working for you and with you. You taught me a great deal about running a business, developing rapport, maintaining decorum. And you made sure I learned from the most qualified and innovative people in the business. I'm grateful for the opportunities you've offered me."

"And I'm sorry it ended on a bad note." He shook her hand, regret and remorse shading his features. "That is, unless you return and help us bring Evensong back to the top-quality spa it was under your direction."

"You're leaving?"

Cam's voice cut in from the side room. He stood there, shoulders back, head high, looking as though she'd just confirmed his worst suspicions.

"Cam, I—"

"I'll see myself out." Kevin turned toward the front door, nodded to Dana, and left.

Dana exited through the kitchen door, leaving Cam and Meredith alone.

Words escaped her. She stood rooted to the soft carpet, not knowing what to say. How to explain.

Cam withdrew a newspaper from the nearby table top. "This is what you wanted to tell me, isn't it?"

Shame cut. "Yes."

"That you fell in love with a guy who pretended to be someone else. Who cheated on his wife, broke his vows, disgraced his kids, and lied his way through multiple affairs, if the national news reports this morning are to be trusted."

Meredith hadn't gone near a news station. "There are more?"

"Three so far. It seems Charles employed the girl-in-every-port mentality."

Meredith sank onto the couch. "I can't believe I was so stupid. That I believed him."

He stayed where he was, watching her. Probably totally disgusted. "You weren't alone."

"That doesn't make it better."

"You loved him."

She frowned. "I thought I did. And it seemed so glamorous at the time. A boyfriend that traveled the world, handsome and smart. Successful. Quick to spend money." She stared at her hands before shrugging. "Stupid."

"I'd say naive."

"Semantics, Cam."

"So."

He moved halfway across the room and took a seat in the chair opposite her. Not next to her, she noted, although the sofa offered plenty of room. A telling move.

"You're leaving."

"Kevin offered me my job back."

"He was your boss in Maryland?"

She nodded. "Yes. And Evensong Resort plays a part in

what I didn't get a chance to tell you. I had broken things off with Chas when I found out he was married. The internet's an amazing thing, and I stumbled onto a picture of him and Sylvia that popped up even without his full name. I couldn't believe my eyes. So then I researched, realized I'd been duped and dumb, and broke things off."

She paused, wishing she could spiral time backward, wanting to even the playing field, clean her soul, but Cam had lived the sweet life of husband. Father. Widower. And she had no right to mess things up for him.

"Continue."

She looked up. He sat just out of reach, watching her, but he didn't look disgusted. Or disdainful. Sad, yes. Concerned. But not reviled, so that was good. "I kept working until last summer when Kevin's daughter approached me. She'd found out about Chas, who he was, what I'd done, and she told me she wanted my job, that she'd do whatever proved necessary to get it. Including going public with my affair with Charles Bellwater." Meredith paused, remembering the conversation. Jude Anne's triumph. Her derision. "Evensong Resort doesn't embrace scandal. I knew if she tipped the press, I'd be done anyway. So I left quietly. Came home. And you know the rest."

She waited, wishing she could paint a better picture of her actions, but that pristine portrait didn't exist. But it could and would. She'd decided that long ago. And despite Cam's look of compassion, she'd lived in the southern part of Allegany County long enough to know that some folks would have a field day with this new discovery. Her immoral actions would spur old talk and new speculation, the two things she hated most. The things that had pushed her from home long ago.

Cam leaned forward, hands clasped. "I loved my wife."

Meredith knew that. It showed in the way he talked of her, the care he gave those girls, the shadow of pain in his gaze when memories piqued him.

"We worked so well together. I was serious, she liked to play. I worked doggedly, she gave me rest. I was totally certain we weren't ready for family and commitments, and then she got pregnant."

"Those things have a tendency to happen in a young marriage."

Cam regarded her with his usual calm. "Sophie was born seven months after our wedding."

"Oh."

He nodded. "Yeah. 'Oh.' And I didn't think I was ready, but that's because I have this stick-in-the-mud personality that gets in the way sometimes."

"Whereas I'd say solid. And caring. And dependable."

He didn't smile in agreement. His gaze rejected the affirming words. "Kristy got sick a few years later. Sophie was in preschool, Rachel was a toddler, they were always catching things. And every time she caught a cold, Rachel would get this really bad cough. Nasty sounding."

Meredith nodded, unsure where he was going, but the pained look on his face said he didn't revisit these days often.

"Kristy developed an awful cough, too, just like Rachel's. It was worse at night, and she felt bad about waking me because I was working on a school house project and finishing a summer job that ran into time delays. Kristy was home with the girls, so our finances depended on my income and that summer job contract wouldn't be paid in full until it was complete and passed the Landmark Society's inspection. Summer gets tight for teachers financially, so I was playing catch-up each week. When Kristy got sick, she decided I needed to sleep and so she left our room and went out to sleep on the couch."

"Because she was concerned for you, Cam."

He grimaced. "No, because I'd gone off on the whole family that day, yelling about how I had so much to do, that I was overwhelmed, and a good night's sleep once in a while would be appreciated."

Guilt and disgust marked his face. Pain shadowed deeper circles beneath his eyes. He clasped his hands and moved closer. "She died that night. All alone, sleeping on the couch, so that I could get my sleep. And for the longest time I couldn't forgive myself for letting that happen."

God help him. Help me. Tell me what to say, what to do. Please.

No words came, nothing of import, anyway. How could she address his guilt and angst when he couldn't come to terms with it himself?

He stood.

So did she.

"But lately, I've been realizing that maybe it's not all about me. Or my mistakes. That if I believe in God, in Christ, in the word, then I have to accept that I'm not always in charge. That sometimes I have to let go. Step back."

"And that's not easy for you."

"Or you." His face softened with a slight smile. "We've both messed up, Mere."

"Cam, no, you can't possibly equate what happened to Kristy, with—"

He cupped her cheek with one hand, quieting her. "I thought God didn't measure mistakes."

She frowned.

He trailed his finger lightly to her cheek, her jaw. "Whither thou goest, I will go. And whither thou lodgest, I will lodge. And thy people shall be my people, Mere."

Did he mean…?

The warm look in his eyes said yes.

His kiss confirmed it.

"Cam…"

"Meredith, if you decide to go back to Maryland, to take

that job, then the girls and I will follow you. Dog your steps. Shadow you. Because you got away from me once."

She nodded and bit her lip, quick tears of joy stinging her eyes.

"And I refuse to let that happen again. I learned the hard way we don't know the day or the hour."

"No." She shook her head in agreement.

"So I'm not in the mind of wasting time, ever again. Will you marry me, Meredith? Share my life, my kids, my ups and downs and my stick-in-the-mud ways?"

She couldn't believe this was happening, really happening. That Cam had come here, knowing what happened in Maryland. He'd bared his soul and proposed.

"You'd really come to Maryland with me?"

He gave her that point-blank studious stare she loved so much. "I believe I made that clear."

So Cam-like. So…perfect.

"Does it sweeten the deal if I say that I don't ever want to go back to Evensong Resort in this lifetime? That I've had enough of backdoor politics and high-income drama to last forever? That all I want to do is open Stillwaters and grow old with you, all the days of my life?"

He grinned, grabbed her into a longer, lingering kiss, then turned her around. "Better yet, come on, grab your jacket. It's crazy cold out there for April."

"Because?"

"We've got to tell the girls, your mother, my mother…"

He tugged her closer as a voice called from the kitchen, "I'm good! I've been listening and you did quite well, Cameron, if I do say so myself. And of course you'll let me help with the planning end, right?"

Meredith met Cam's gaze with a silent promise of tomorrow. "How fast can you plan, Mom?"

Dana bustled through the door, her laptop in hand. "I've already drawn up the guest lists we used for the boys' weddings, so we've got a head start. You guys give me a date when you get done kissing, and we'll go from there."

"Will the White Church at the Bend be in good shape by August?"

"Should be." Dana nodded, matter-of-fact and purposeful, tapping keys the moment she sat. "Matt and his father-in-law have a crew lined up to do the roofing and plaster work once the weather dries up."

"Can Reverend Hannity join in with Simon?" Cam asked.

"Love 'em both, so yes," Meredith agreed. "If they've got time. And in all seriousness, Cam?" Meredith cradled his face and kissed him gently. "I'd marry you tomorrow with no pomp and circumstance required."

"Then…"

"But——" she flicked him a grin, grabbed her jacket, and headed for the door, pulling him along "——there are two little girls who would love a chance to be in a wedding, I expect. And a few months will give me time to get to know them better. And build a better relationship with your mother. And open a spa. And…"

He laughed, waved to Dana, and followed his future bride through the door. "I get it. But just so you know." He stopped her forward progress and drew her in for one more drawn-out, love-you-so-much kiss. "I will be a wonderful husband to you, Meredith."

A smile and a sheen of tears mixed her expression. "I know. And I'll give the whole family free haircuts, totally a win/win."

He sighed as she dropped her head to his chest, the feel of holding her, loving her, filling his heart. Calming his soul.

She was on the phone before he put the car in gear, checking her calendar with Pastor Simon, throwing out dates, figuring out how to squeeze in a wedding between soccer tournaments, his summer job at the new cooperative and the opening of Stillwaters.

Listening to her, he realized her fears of being like her father were unwarranted. Meredith Brennan was her mother's daughter, a gentle, trusting, hardworking soul that simply wanted to do a good job.

And he couldn't wait to get started on that together.

* * * * *

Dear Reader,

I love this story of Meredith and Cam's reunion, their second chance. Teenage love is filled with the tempest of the moment, the hour, the day. It's a high-energy time, ripe with expectations.

Mature love sees beyond the romance and takes the chance anyway, knowing that faith, hope and love abide. Cam's story was based on a glimpse into Southern Tier life afforded me by a seatmate on my plane ride from Orlando to Rochester, New York. She told me of a teacher who goes beyond…a shop teacher who buys old buildings and uses their refurbishing to teach his class life skills. AWESOME!

Meredith? She's based on a local gal who lived her dream, despite being advised against it. Jackie Fridd Leturneau was a smart teen who wanted to do hair. She was advised to go to college and make something of herself. Her family disagreed, because shouldn't we all be able to make money doing what we love?

In 1993 the family started a small salon. Jackie's mother Judy was on board, and soon her sister Jennifer joined the group. Together, these three women built a business that necessitated a move in seven short years. Nine years later they built a 10,000-square-foot spa and salon, offering warm and engaging services to upstate New York. Their story, their success, became Meredith Brennan's work story. I love women who go outside the norm to achieve their dreams, and when I was first introduced to Solutions Studio and Spa in Rochester (by my beautiful daughter-in-law Lacey), I was amazed by what these gals had done.

Life isn't always easy. Life demands choices and change. In Meredith's case it meant owning bad choices. In Cam's it meant dealing with guilt and moving on. But with God's help, with his direction, our past can become the floorboards of the present. Something to stand on and learn from, no more, no less.

I hope you enjoy this story of forging a new family, right here in Allegany County, New York!

Ruthy

Questions for Discussion

1. Meredith Brennan has returned to Allegany County for a fresh start, a new beginning. "Coming home" after a long absence can be exhilarating and scary. Have you ever had to return to an old place, an old time? Was the return easy? Why or why not?

2. Meredith is clearly ashamed of her past and regrets her actions. Do you think it would be easy to get swept up in a fast-paced lifestyle when surrounded by well-to-do people? Does that make it easier to excuse your actions?

3. Cam Calhoun has a lot on his plate. He's put God on a back burner, convinced that he and God both let his late wife down. Have you ever had a time when it was hard to see God's plan? Or be convinced that He existed?

4. Cam's girls are typical sisters in so many ways, but he's confused about how to handle them. In his determination to raise them the way Kristy would have, he negates their femininity. How do parents draw a good line between excess importance on looks and understanding that it's okay to look good?

5. Evelyn Calhoun was a fun character to work with. Her grumpiness is deep-seated but I loved seeing her gradual turnaround. Have you ever had an emotionally or physically difficult time be the catalyst for better understanding and greater faith?

6. Dana Brennan is a survivor. She hides her hurt with determination and faith. Do you know people like Dana,

people who have a tendency to overcome whatever life puts in their path? How does your faith help you when things go wrong?

7. Meredith left Allegany County as a teen from a dysfunctional family. Unfortunately, her family's standing in the community put her father's misdeeds in the limelight. When faced with the same thing fourteen years later, faith and maturity help her through. Has your faith grown with you? Has that walk been step-by-step? Why or why not?

8. Sophie and Rachel have a longing for feminine things, but they hide that wistfulness to protect their father's feelings. Have you ever seen a child assume the role of the protector, longing for their parent's happiness?

9. The quest and worry for Sally the kitten illustrates Cam's dogged determination to get the job done, sometimes forgetting the importance of little things. Do you know any single parents? Is it hard for them to find the time to relax when they're so busy paying the bills? Raising the kids? How could you help with that?

10. Meredith knows her past is going to bite her present. Fear that she's not good enough for Cam makes her hold back. Does your faith help you to face your fears? Does it give you strength to face the day?

11. Cam's moment of truth comes when he realizes his work ethic has messed up another holiday. And when he realizes Rachel's longing from a computer screen, he gets the much needed smack-upside-the-head. Has the Holy Spirit ever given you a wake-up call? Nudged you into a new opportunity?

12. Meredith opens up to her mother and Heather when she realizes time is running short. How did this push of honesty help thrust her forward? Have you ever experienced the Biblical reality of "the truth shall set you free"?

13. Evelyn's cancer diagnosis sets the stage for consternation, worry and healing. Her relationship with Cam is improved partially because he reaches out physically by hugging and kissing her and emotionally by scouting out alternative treatments for her. His firm step forward helped to meet him halfway. Why is it so hard to be the first one to break a standoff?

14. Meredith refuses to hide when the reporters come to town to chase down her story. How does standing our ground help develop our inner character?

15. Cam comes to terms with his past and Meredith's reasons for leaving as a teenager. He realizes she's in a similar predicament now. Is it brave or foolhardy for him to declare his love and offer to follow her?

REQUEST YOUR FREE BOOKS!

2 FREE INSPIRATIONAL NOVELS
PLUS 2
FREE
MYSTERY GIFTS

Love Inspired

Love Inspired

‹— TEXAS TWINS —›

Follow the adventures of two sets of twins who are torn apart by family secrets and learn to find their way home.

Her Surprise Sister by Marta Perry
July 2012

Mirror Image Bride by Barbara McMahon
August 2012

Carbon Copy Cowboy by Arlene James
September 2012

Look-Alike Lawman by Glynna Kaye
October 2012

The Soldier's Newfound Family
by Kathryn Springer
November 2012

Reunited for the Holidays
by Jillian Hart
December 2012

*Available wherever
books are sold.*

www.LoveInspiredBooks.com

LICONT0812